WASTE OF WORTH

DELUCA DUET: PART ONE

BETHANY-KRIS

Published by Bethany-Kris

www.bethanykris.com

eISBN 13: 978-1-988197-27-2
Print ISBN 13: 978-1-988197-26-5

Cover Art © Jay Aheer
Editor: Nina S. Gooden

DEDICATION

For my readers. For your love and your loyalty. I hope Dino is everything
you wanted and so much more.

TABLE OF
CONTENTS

CHAPTER 1

MEMORIES could make a monster out of a man.

There were times that seemed harder to deal with than others; passing moments that could make Dino DeLuca's chest tighten in pain, or his fists clench in anger.

The sound of metal being dropped was one of the worst. He swore he could feel his back bruising and bleeding all over again at the simple tinging tone.

Whispered words made him jumpy—*paranoid*. Whispers were good for nothing but taunting, and he didn't want to hear those mocking words anymore.

Had enough yet?

Learn to follow directions, Dino.

It should fucking hurt, kid.

The stench of vomit, clinging to the air and seemingly never letting go, would make his panic rush into overdrive, overwhelming him with an almost-sense of itchiness all over his skin. As if the vomit was still soaked and dripping off his clothes in the darkness as he sobbed in a dank basement, curled in a corner and fighting off another round of sickness.

The reactions always came so swiftly that they surprised him, no matter the time or place. His memories weren't much different when it came right down to it.

These times were the most difficult for Dino.

Those times came at night.

When the lights were off …

When the apartment was quiet …

When it was just him and his monsters …

When he was alone.

The most frightening thing about monsters was the fact that they could be anybody. The old man sitting outside the pizzeria, tipping his hat at the ladies passing by. The young woman on the city bus with her hair bleached white and her gaze distant, staring at anything *but* anyone. The mother pushing a stroller down the street, oblivious but focused.

Or a monster could be the man dressed in three-piece suit stepping out of the restaurant he owns, the ring of the key fob for his white Bentley spinning circles as he whistled *Ave Maria* on his way to church.

Dino caught sight of the lower portion of his reflection in the darkly tinted glass of his Bentley's window.

He managed a smile.

It was more like a smirk.

Fact was, the expression he wore was neither. Dino found it incredibly hard to smile—something that came so easy for others was foreign to him. When he did try, it came off as a grimacing grin and that worked its way into a sneer.

Or a smirk.

He liked that better.

It was *manageable*.

The monster was *definitely* the man wearing the three-piece suit with the key fob in his hand, staring at himself in the window, Dino knew.

Slipping into the SUV, the noise of the busy Chicago city street was instantly silenced. Dino turned on his vehicle and checked his rearview mirror before he pulled out onto the road.

He regretted choosing the rearview almost immediately.

While his reflection in the window of his car had been partly obscured by the shadows of trees providing shade to the sidewalk, it was not concealed at all in the rearview mirror.

Dino didn't like mirrors.

He didn't like the face staring back at him.

The soulless brown gaze, emotionless expression, and silence were more than enough to make him look away.

Except he couldn't.

Under the right edge of his strong jaw was a three-inch scar that started three-quarters of the way up his throat and stopped just before his ear. The broad slope of his nose had the slightest crook in the middle. Sometimes the left side of his jaw ached when it rained.

Those were the obvious things—marks, scars, and reminders he could pick out instantly when faced with his reflection. The longer he stared at himself, the more he would find.

It was—without meaning to be—the most dangerous game he could play with himself.

Church, he told himself. *You need to be seen at church.*

It was only the ringing of his phone that finally drove his gaze away from the rearview mirror, making him check the caller ID, and breaking his cycle of self-loathing.

Dino was grateful for that.

Not so much the caller that interrupted him.

Sighing, he connected the call through Bluetooth as he pulled out onto the road.

"DeLuca here," Dino answered.

"Why the *fuck* is Riley Conti calling me with demands about *you*, Dino?"

Dino silently counted back from five before he answered his younger brother. "Theo, good morning to you, too. Are you at church? I'm headed that way. We can talk then."

"Dino—"

"Church, man."

Dino let the call drop.

Theo wouldn't say two words to Dino at the church and he knew it for a fact. When it came to the public, Theo and Dino were constantly apart from one another—on opposite sides of the room where they didn't have to speak.

It was the easiest way for Dino to handle Theo DeLuca.

Maybe that made him a coward.

The brothers' history together was not an easy one, not when it had been shadowed by the death of their parents, and then the events that followed the murders. Unlike Dino, who learned quickly that trust was a beautiful myth in their lifestyle and in the Chicago Outfit, Theo was of a more stubborn mindset.

And so, the two were distant.

Dino tried with Theo, but it never really seemed to help the relationship.

He was all too aware that his younger brother blamed him for things that had been out of his control, though Theo thought his older sibling could have handled the past far better.

He probably could have—*should* have.

Dino thought he had, honestly. He'd taken years of abuse from the hands of their uncle Ben after their parents' deaths. He'd lived separately from the family, sure, but he was not exempt from the beatings or the manipulation.

Of course, that was a story for another day.

If Dino got his wish, that day would never come.

Another call rang through to Dino's cell phone.

He checked the caller ID again.

Ben DeLuca, it read.

Dino didn't pick up the call, still driving toward the church.

He would see Ben soon enough.

Without even being told, Dino was already aware he would suffer for not picking up the call.

Years had passed since he'd suffered some form of physical harm from his uncle's hard hand.

Years.

Dino's chest tightened at the thought.

Truth was, he still wasn't exempt from the manipulation.

Not when he was constantly haunted with it all.

He still wasn't free.

Dino slid quietly into the church pew less than five minutes after Mass had started for the parishioners. He avoided meeting the gazes of those he recognized, uninterested in a whispered conversation while the priest was preaching respect from behind his pulpit at the altar.

Of course, his hope didn't last long before Ben DeLuca made his way over, sitting just a seat behind Dino.

Church was supposed to be Dino's safe place.

It was meant for God—not men.

Ben had never been very good at following those rules.

"You're late," Ben said.

The priest continued on from the front, his sermon about respect likely being lost on the majority listening.

Dino was not one of those people.

He understood *respect* far better than most.

So, even though he hated his uncle—while he despised the man and the hell he'd caused in Dino's life from the murder of his parents to the abuse of himself and his siblings—he didn't shun Ben when he spoke.

He answered back.

He followed the rules.

Always.

"Traffic," Dino lied.

Knowing Ben wouldn't see it, Dino glanced up at the vaulted ceiling, sending off a silent apology to God. It had to be double the sin to lie in church, surely.

It wasn't the first time.

"You didn't answer my call earlier," Ben said.

Dino stiffened slightly, but managed to hide the action by shifting a bit in the pew to make it seem as though he were searching for a better position. "I was on another call—Theo, actually. By the time I was done, I was practically here."

Ben seemed to let it pass.

Seemed being the keyword.

"Yes, your brother is in a fit, though he didn't want to talk about why," Ben muttered more to himself than Dino.

"Riley."

That was all Dino really needed to say, and he knew his uncle would get the hint. Theo, a young, made soldier in their mafia family—much like Dino had been before getting his Capo title—sometimes had a problem with authority. Although he knew to follow the rules. Mostly, he did that well.

Given the fact that Riley Conti was the front boss for the Chicago Outfit, he often got the majority say where the Capos and the business were concerned on the streets. While the main boss, Terrance Trentini, and the underboss, Dino's uncle, made the calls for the family as a whole.

It was all a delicate business, really.

Four factions of Capos made up the crews, with Dino heading

the DeLuca side of things. The Rossis handled business at the top of Chicago, working alongside the Trentini family, while the DeLucas were at the bottom of Chicago, running business against the territory lines of the Conti family.

Delicate, yes.

Sometimes, the families—the Capos, really—didn't work well together.

Sometimes they were a breath away from killing each other.

Sometimes Theo had to work with people he would rather bury.

It didn't help that Theo didn't particularly care for Riley Conti and hadn't for quite a while. And for good reason. Who would care for a man who once nearly beat him to death with a metal chair over a simple disagreement?

That had been years ago, but it still happened.

Theo didn't let shit go.

Not that Dino blamed him.

"Well, handle that," Ben finally said, bringing Dino from his thoughts. "We have a meeting coming up and the last thing I want to do is listen to Theo and Riley bark at one another again."

Dino nodded, his gaze sweeping through the people in the pews to find his younger brother. He didn't bother to explain that Riley was actually bothering Theo about him, because Ben wouldn't give a shit about that fact. He didn't care that Riley enjoyed bothering Theo, simply because he could, or that he took shots at the young soldier's age like he didn't deserve to be where he was—or the button into the family that he had earned—if only because he was younger than most in the position.

Theo was good at his job. He worked under his older brother with the goal of having the actual Capo title. He helped to manage the DeLuca crew, and other than the bosses above them, the only person he really had to answer to now was Dino.

He fucking deserved the credit for that.

But ...

Outfit men were bastards.

Each and every single one of them.

"I'll get whatever little dispute they're having handled," Dino assured, never once giving his uncle his full attention.

It was easier this way.

Easier for him to pretend like all he had time for where Ben was concerned were passing moments and a quick, quiet conversation.

That way, he wasn't letting Ben in.

Not close enough to hurt him again, or to find something to take from him.

Ben liked that too much.

He'd already taken enough.

"Oh, and before I forget," Ben said as he stood.

Dino grinded his molars when he felt Ben's hand land on his shoulder. The older man's fingers squeezed tightly, and while it didn't hurt, it certainly make every muscle in Dino's body freeze like blocks of ice.

The touch was meant to be affectionate.

A nice gesture between an uncle and a nephew.

It only made Dino *sick*.

"What is it?" Dino asked.

Ben released his hold, but patted Dino's shoulder. "Happy birthday. I nearly forgot—Carmela reminded me. You should celebrate tonight, but not too much, Dino. Business first, my boy. Business always comes first."

Dino didn't thank Ben for the well wishes, but his uncle was already walking away, heading back for his own pew where his wife was sitting with a bible open in her hands.

It was a little strange. Maybe even sad.

He hadn't necessarily forgotten his birthday, but he didn't care to remember it, either. It was just another year of life—twenty-nine all together.

Dino didn't understand why he should celebrate his life when he was barely fucking living it.

CHAPTER 2

EVERYONE had choices to make that would eventually lead their lives down one path or another. And sometimes, making one choice could lead to a separate set of roadblocks that would then lead them into yet another set of choices, often more difficult ones.

Dino understood this better than most.

At thirteen years old, he'd make a choice to get involved with a group of boys that liked nothing more than to cause a little trouble. He was accustomed to trouble, liked it even. He'd grown up seeing his father making money by the trouble he caused, and so it only seemed like the next logical step for Dino to follow in those footsteps.

Joseph DeLuca had, of course, denied his son.

Dino had decided, all those years ago, that he really didn't need his father's permission to do what he wanted to do, and so the group of boys came into play.

That was his first choice.

It led him into a world of thieves and ground-runners.

Thugs stealing whatever was available and then selling it for cheap on the streets. Others ran for the drug dealers, doing errands or making drop-offs when they were needed for some extra cash, on the hope that it would lead to a better position in the crew.

God knew Dino hadn't needed to dabble in any of those things—there was more than enough of it inside his own family, for Christ's sake. His father had been an Outfit Capo, right alongside his uncle.

The drugs Dino was helping the dealers to drop?

It came from *his* family.

Eventually, his uncle Ben had urged him toward the mafia more than the streets, much to his father's chagrin and protest. He started learning about that *world*, that crazy, private, suffocating world that surrounded his family in secrecy, rules, and demands.

By the time he was sixteen, Dino knew exactly what he wanted to be.

A made man.

It was such a strange thing, he knew, how the very same choices he had made eventually shaped him, were the same ones his father had been faced with growing up, but they had led Joseph down an entirely different path.

One that included eventual death.

Dino remembered the day he'd moved out of his parents' Melrose Park home like it was yesterday. His mother had kept her back turned to him the whole time. Not out of anger or disgust, but because she was crying and she didn't want him to see it. Valerie DeLuca loved all three of her children, no matter their choices or mistakes, but she sided with her husband on the off-chance that Dino would stay.

He hadn't.

His father packed his bags.

Go back to school, drop this Outfit nonsense, and you can come home, his father had told him at the door.

The only thing that made Dino pause was his sister Lily and his brother Theo. He looked after them, because despite how hypocritical his father was with his demands for Dino to live a *clean* life while he was busy making dirty money, he cared for his siblings.

But little Lily had Theo.

So ... Dino made another choice.

Nearly a year later, to the very day he'd moved out, his parents were murdered in that quaint little Melrose Park home. His father, shot in the face as he sat at the kitchen table, and his mother in the back of the head as she ran for the front door.

It'd been a fucking *bloodbath*.

Dino had only seen the aftermath, weeks later when the blood on the walls was dried and the red puddles on the yellow-tiled floor had turned to crusted stains. He'd gone back in the house to get things of his and his siblings'—memories for them when they were older and they wouldn't be able to remember their mother and father all too well.

The police hadn't cleaned it up.

It wasn't their job, apparently.

Despite how he'd left the relationship with his parents, strained and distant, he still loved them. The last thing he wanted was for the memories that his siblings had to be turned into something *foul*.

The whispers and rumors had begun damn near instantly.

Joseph was a rat, feeding police with inside information as to their business and the inner workings of the Chicago mob like he had every right. He'd gotten what he deserved.

Dino never argued his father's fate—never once spoke against the people who said Joseph earned the punishment that put him in the ground. And despite learning that it was Joseph's own brother to pull the trigger—Ben, that was—Dino's only desire was to protect his siblings from a similar fate.

Traitors ate bullets.

Simple as that.

But that didn't mean he liked it.

Or that it didn't fill him with rage every time he considered his mother being caught up in it all.

Valerie had been an innocent, stuck in a mess of her husband's making, a man she loved, yes, but not one she was able to protect. Like most mafia wives, she was born into the lifestyle with a father and grandfather who had been gangsters, and she married a man just like them because that was what she had been taught to do. She raised her family from home, never working or asking for more than what her husband provided because women of the mafia were expected *not* to complain if they wanted to keep their husbands at home, in their bed and their place.

Dino remembered his mother being sweet—loving her husband and her family.

She only died that night because she'd opted to stay in with Joseph, instead of taking one of her very infrequent ladies' nights that had been pre-planned.

Sighing, Dino wished all of this past shit was easier for him to deal with, but it wasn't. It was these choices, both those he made himself and those made by his father, that led him to the hell that was Ben DeLuca.

Maybe he hated the dead man a little for it.

Not his mother, though.

Never her.

Bending down in front of the gravestone, Dino pulled the pristine white handkerchief from his suit pocket, and began wiping the bits of dirt and blades of grass from the front of the shiny marker. He read his mother's name, and took in the dates she had lived and died.

He always tried to stop by whenever Sunday rolled around.

Guilt was a silent killer.

Dino couldn't help but wonder if he had stayed, if he had done what his mother and father wanted all those years ago, would she have been spared? Would she have been home, or gone like she was supposed to be?

Would he have died, too?

She was the innocent one.

He was filthy like his father.

Why did those who deserved angel wings earn them far faster than those who didn't?

"Lily's gone to Europe," Dino said to the gravestone, tucking the cloth back into his pocket. "She was pretty determined to go, Ma, and I didn't want her around here more than she needed to be. I love her—she needs to be happy, right?"

It'd taken years, but Dino finally had the control over his siblings that he'd fought for where his uncle Ben and aunt Carmela were concerned. After the death of his parents, Ben had beaten Dino black and blue that very same night when he thought to take his brother and sister with him to be cared for.

Ben couldn't have that—he wanted *control*.

Control of the DeLuca name, of the children left behind that he could shape and mold, and of the teenaged boy he'd already been slowly moving away from his father.

Ben wanted all of that, and he'd gotten it.

That was the first time Dino learned Ben was not to be trusted.

The second time was worse than the first ...

"Anyway, she's happy, and keeps sending me postcards with pictures," Dino explained.

To some it probably seemed stupid for him to talk to a grave. His mother's body had long rotted away in a casket six feet under,

17

and her soul was gone high above, likely.

But it *helped*.

Very few things helped Dino.

Knowing he had to go and chat with Riley Conti for the sake of peace and business, Dino said a quiet goodbye to his mother, giving the headstone one more pat with his hand before he stood straight. Dino fixed his jacket as he weaved in and out of the other markers, careful not to step on the graves as that was just disrespectful to the dead.

And he'd kill any fucking fool who stepped on his mother's grave.

He'd just stepped onto the stone pathway heading back toward the parking lot of the church when something rammed back into him from behind.

The quiet *ommpf* sound was followed by a quick apology.

"Sorry!"

Dino spun on his heel, coming face to face with a young woman that held a large camera in her hands and eyes so wide he was pretty sure he would be able to see his reflection in the brown depths if he looked hard enough. She was pretty—beautiful, even—in an unassuming way, with her earth-toned clothing and her long, caramel-colored hair tied up in a messy bun at the very top of her head. The sunglasses on her head fell down over her face, hiding those eyes of hers, as she took another step backward.

She pushed the sunglasses back to the crown of her head.

Dino was still staring at her, quite unsure of what to do.

"You okay?" he asked.

The woman nodded, smiling just a bit.

That led his attention to the gentle curve of her pink lips, and the way her shoulder lifted at the same time.

"My fault," she replied. "I was walking backward to get the right shot—missed you coming out from behind the statue. Nice day for photos, though, so I couldn't help myself. I get the best ones in the cemeteries."

Dino's brow furrowed.

She talked a lot.

He barely talked at all, even when he was forced into conversation.

Maybe that was why he felt so awkward standing there, unsure of what to say or *if* she even wanted him to.

"I saw you, though," the girl continued. "Over there, right?"

She pointed back toward his mother's grave.

Dino just blinked. "Uh."

She didn't seem the slightest bit put off by his lack of communication, instead, rolling right on with whatever she had to say next.

"It makes me curious when I'm photographing cemeteries and see people talking to graves or whatever, and I almost stop them to chat, but never do. It wouldn't be right."

Yet, there she was, talking to him.

That was not lost on Dino.

She stuck her hand out, offering it to him.

"Karen Martin," she said.

Dino's gaze flicked down at her hand, and without his permission, lifted his own to take hers. There was a warmth to her skin that wasn't in his, he noticed. They were both outside, so there was no real reason for the temperature difference.

Karen smiled widely. "You should tell me your name, it's only fair."

"Dino," he said, surprised at how quietly his name came out.

"Do you come here often?"

Again, he answered, more honestly than perhaps he should have spoken. "Once a week usually to visit my mother."

That brightness in her features dimmed just a bit, but she still managed a smile.

Dino couldn't help but notice that it was a beautiful smile.

Even when it was sad.

"Can I make a confession, Dino?" Karen asked.

Dino eyed her, both curious and a little wary of her sunny disposition while she stood chatting happily in the middle of a cemetery with a man she didn't know from Adam.

"Go for it, Karen."

"Me bumping into you wasn't really an accident," she said with a wink. "You looked sad—I wanted to see if I could make you smile."

He wasn't quite sure what to make of that.

Karen shrugged her one shoulder again, letting go of his hand and pointing at his face as she took a step backward. "And you are, Dino. Smiling, I mean."

Was he?

Karen laughed, a sweet sound that reminded him of a melody, floating in the wind and being carried further away. "Have a great day, Dino. And if you need to smile next Sunday, I might be around."

Before he could reply, Karen was already gone back up the pathway, and disappearing behind a rather large statue in the cemetery.

It took two minutes for Dino to get back to his car.

His reflection in the driver's window confirmed Karen's statement.

He *was* smiling.

How strange ...

CHAPTER 3

"FOR the *sake* of business?" Theo snarled.

Dino barely passed his younger brother a glance at his show of anger—it wasn't unusual for Theo, as far as that went. "We all have to play nice with people we don't like, Theo."

"Riley Conti is a fucking—"

"Cool it," Dino interrupted, finally giving his brother his attention. "We're in the middle of a fucking church parking lot. The least you could do is keep your tantrum at a quiet level so that we're not sharing our problems with the goddamn neighbors. It's not like they need more to gossip about where the Outfit is concerned."

"Right, that's what you're worried about, not the fact that Riley is a cocksucker who can't be trusted. Let's jump in bed with the snakes, huh? Sure."

"Theo—"

"Fuck you, Dino."

With that last statement, his brother pushed off the side of the vehicle and stalked off, heading toward his own car down the lot.

Dino stared up at the sky, wishing for patience. He wasn't exactly surprised at how the conversation had gone with Theo, as this was how it usually went whenever they had to discuss things. *Especially* if Dino had to put restrictions on his brother's business in some shape or form.

The week had been *hell*.

He'd done his business as he was supposed to, and worked out a deal that Riley would be happy with, but one that Theo would not be pleased about having to contribute to. Because the Conti and DeLuca territory lines were so close together, it only made sense for the families to work together when needed.

Unfortunately, that meant Theo, being the leader of the crew on the streets, would need to answer to Riley at times when business intermingled.

It was a shitty situation, but required.

He didn't know what else to tell his brother.

Theo would have to suck it up.

Dino was forced to work with Ben DeLuca every day of his life, and he despised that man with all the fibers of his being.

Nobody said being a made man was fun or easy.

It was far from it.

Frustrated but refusing to show it, Dino headed toward the cemetery, wanting to check his mother's grave and update her on the week.

Right, he thought, *and that is it.*

It certainly wasn't to see if Karen was there again, like she had promised to be, taking pictures and making him *smile*.

He certainly hadn't thought about her at all or their brief encounter.

He most definitely wasn't curious about her.

Dino didn't have time for those sorts of things. His life didn't allow for things that made him smile or gave him a reprieve from the constant darkness shadowing it, not even a brown-eyed stranger with a soft smile and a sweet laugh.

Absolutely *not*.

And yet, as Dino stepped into the cemetery just beyond the iron gates and large stone wall that was too high to see over, the very first thing he did look for was Karen. He didn't know the woman at all, and while he'd been tempted to see if he could find out more about a Chicagoan photographer that went by the name Karen, he opted not to.

Dino didn't make an effort to have relationships of any sort. Not romantic, or even friendly. They never ended well, and he wasn't the type, frankly. He didn't have the time or care for it.

But even if he did ... a thick fear curled around his throat like a noose, threatening to strangle him with the force of the invisible feeling.

He couldn't afford love of any kind.

Like everything else, it would only be taken away.

It didn't matter, it seemed.

Karen was nowhere to be seen in the cemetery.

Ignoring the heaviness settling in his gut at the realization, Dino made his way to his mother's grave. He spent a good ten minutes there, cleaning off her stone and talking quietly. It was only when he stood and turned to leave did he pause.

Karen stood far back, sitting on a stone bench with the camera in her hands once again. She raised it, and snapped a picture of him before calling out, "I was a little bit late today."

Dino found himself smiling again. "Oh?"

"Traffic is a bitch."

He laughed, taken off-guard at her crass candor.

"No pictures today then?" he asked, walking toward her.

Karen glanced down at the camera, focusing on the screen as she pressed a button over and over. "I got the ones I wanted."

Dino didn't ask her for more information, instead, taking a seat beside her on the bench. "Why cemeteries?"

"Sundays are for cemeteries. Mondays are for birds and trees. Tuesdays are for people. See where I'm going with this?"

He did.

"Whatever catches your attention, huh?"

"Pretty much," Karen said. "Of course, I have to feed myself and pay the rent on my loft, so the majority of my time is spent on people who *pay*."

"Interesting."

"You don't sound interested," Karen noted.

He was.

More than he could explain.

More than what was safe.

Quickly, Dino stood from the bench, brushing invisible dust from the arms of his suit. "Have a wonderful—"

"Did I say something wrong?"

He didn't know how to explain it to her, but it wasn't her that was wrong.

"No, but I have to go. It was nice seeing you again."

Pleasant.

Cold.

Distant.

Dino didn't know how to be any other way. He didn't let

people close because they didn't stay that way for long. He didn't think it was fair for them to be hurt because he was weak. He was far better at being alone, anyway.

No, it certainly wasn't her that was wrong.

It was all him.

Karen was still peering at Dino with curiosity burning brightly in her gaze. "I'll be here again next weekend."

It was then that Dino knew this strange woman was interested in him, for whatever reason. How many times could she photograph the same cemetery?

It didn't matter that he might like to know a bit more about her, too.

Or even why she was curious about him.

He wasn't allowed to have things that made him happy—it had to be given. When he took happiness for himself, it was always ripped away.

"I won't be here," Dino told her.

With that, he walked away.

Ben tipped his glass of whiskey in Dino's direction, giving him a look that said his next statement was not going to be something Dino liked.

"Your sister—call her back from Europe. It's been too long."

Dino used his own bottle of beer to hide the frown starting to form. "I'm not calling Lily back. She's fine over there."

"She needs to be here, Dino. Get her set up in a marriage of good standing."

Absolutely not.

Dino couldn't outright refuse Ben, given he was the head of the DeLuca family, and the Outfit's underboss, but he could use what bit of power he had to divert attention.

"Soon," Dino promised. "I haven't picked someone yet, or even offered."

"Tommas Rossi—"

Dino's teeth grinded, but he managed to interrupt Ben with a quiet but firm, "No."

"Is it Tommas you take issue with, or a Rossi?"

Certainly not the Rossi family.

"Tommas is looking at someone else," Dino said, offering nothing else.

He didn't know if it was true. He had no idea if the Rossi Capo was looking at any woman as a wife, but Dino *did* know it wouldn't be Lily.

"Joel, then," Ben said.

Was that what they were going to do?

Toss out names of men in the Outfit until Ben hit the one Dino would agree to marry his sister off to?

"For now, she's fine where she is," Dino repeated.

Ben didn't look all too pleased, but it was what it was.

Unfortunately, if Ben *really* wanted Lily married off, all he would need to do was make a few phone calls of his own, set up the arrangement, and call her home. Dino wouldn't get much of a say.

And the only say Dino *would* have, was if he ended up being the person to set up Lily in a marriage of his choosing.

She would hate him for that, he knew.

It would be unforgiveable to her.

Dino figured he had a bit of time before he'd have to worry about all of that. A couple of years, hopefully. A whole lifetime to someone of Lily's age, essentially. Maybe when he did finally step in, to save her from having their uncle pick her a husband, she would understand why Dino had been the one to choose.

At least he would pick a man who would love her, care for her, and give her the world.

Maybe he already had a man in mind, but … time.

He had time.

"And Theo," Ben added, resting back in his desk chair.

Dino had all he could do not to roll his eyes. "What about Theo, Ben?"

"Find Theo a wife—he needs the same thing Lily does. It might even settle him down a bit."

The laugh that broke free from Dino's chest was both sardonic and bitter.

"That's never going to happen," Dino told Ben, knowing it was true. "If you want to keep Theo compliant and happy doing what *you* want him to do, then your best bet is to leave him the hell alone. Theo will get married to whoever the fuck he wants, whenever the fuck he wants, and you'll get no say in it all, Ben, so don't waste your time."

Dino knew better than to poke at his uncle in such a way that was almost taunting in nature. Ben had no patience for that, and had zero qualms with reminding Dino of just how powerless he could be against him.

But it had been the truth.

Ben needed to hear it.

"Is that so?" Ben asked.

"I say it for *your* benefit," Dino replied, "not mine. It'd be a headache, and nothing more."

"I suppose that only really leaves us with one person to move our family up in the Outfit, then."

Dino's confusion must have been obvious in his expression, because Ben smiled in that cold way of his, tipping his glass toward his oldest nephew.

"You, Dino." Ben shrugged, taking another drink of whiskey. "That only leaves us with you."

Well ...

"I don't want a wife," Dino said quietly.

Why would he ever want to bring someone into the hell that was the mafia? How selfish of a creature would he be to trap a woman in a life where the next day was not promised and the world that should be safe and happy was constantly in an uproar and unstable?

As for him ...

Dino was a broken man, unable to even sleep at night, and he wasn't even sure he knew how to love a woman properly, let alone give her a happy life.

No, marriage was not in his future.

"Want and need are two very different things. And it isn't about what *you* want or need, Dino, it's about *la famiglia*. That's the problem with the Outfit—when a family is quiet for too long, when they do nothing to better their position, then they fade into the background and are seen as weak. Is that what you want for the DeLuca family—to be a *target*?"

26

In a way, Ben was right.

That was the culture of the Outfit and the families within it.

They were always competing, always fighting. It never ended, though it was tiring.

"How much higher do you want to be exactly?" Dino dared to ask.

Ben eyed him from the side, taking in the question. "I beg your pardon?"

"You said this was to move the family up in the Outfit—*our* family specifically. Exactly how high do you want to be, Ben? You're the underboss, and we both know you have zero interest in running the streets as the front boss like Riley does. So where are we going exactly?"

Ben smiled that cold and familiar sight again.

It made Dino sick.

His uncle always smiled before something bad happened, especially where Dino was concerned. He'd seen that smile too many times to count before he'd ended up in a hospital, making up some lie as to how he'd earned himself another broken bone or one of many bruises.

"We're going up," Ben said. "All the way up, Dino."

"The boss is your friend," Dino replied, referring to the Outfit's leader, Terrance Trentini.

"There is no such thing as friends, Dino. Haven't I taught you that over the years?"

Yes, yes he had.

CHAPTER 4

DINO watched as one season left, and a new one came. He didn't mind the passing time, the days bleeding together and the weeks drifting away before his very eyes. He wasn't the type of person who counted time, unless of course, he had something to wait for.

He hadn't had something like that in ... well, forever.

But with new seasons came new business.

Case in point, the strip club down in the Heights that Ben had finally had enough of, and decided to sign over to Dino for a half-decent price. The Heights was one of the dirtier parts of Chicago, with a higher crime rate, shitty schools, and all the characters that came along with it.

Dino liked it.

If only because he could do nearly all of his transactions from behind the desk in a back office of the strip club as it allowed for little surveillance. All types of people walked in and out of the joint, and no one would blink an eye at the many patrons that slipped into the back offices, with envelopes in hand, after enjoying a show from the girls.

Dino took each and every envelope with a grin-and-bear-it attitude, only counting the money and dispersing the dirty cash where it needed to go when he was alone again. Automatically, seventy percent of anything he made went to the boss of the Outfit. Then, ten percent of his cut went to Ben without question.

He was left with the rest.

It wasn't anything to scoff at, as far as that went.

Add in his many business ventures, from clubs to restaurants, and Dino was doing okay financially. He only wished his many bank accounts, including the several he had offshore to hide funds, would give him some sense of security.

They didn't.

"Hey."

Dino glanced up at his brother's voice, finding Theo leaning in the doorway of the office with his usual scowl in place. Theo always stuck around to keep an eye on the people coming in and out when tribute was coming up and people had to pay their dues. It was the only time the two brothers managed to work well with one another without some sort of fight starting up.

Money could do that to people.

"What do you want?" Dino asked.

"New recruits are waiting for you."

Dino sighed, rubbing at his temples to ease the headache starting to form. He'd slept like shit the night before—frankly, he slept like shit every night—but he was running on less than two hours sleep over a span of several days. It was starting to show, considering he didn't have the slightest fucking clue what Theo was talking about.

"The what?"

"The people who put in applications for the dancing job—strippers, Dino."

Oh.

Yeah, shit.

"How many showed up?"

He'd have to watch a routine from each one. Most men probably wouldn't mind that, getting a free lap dance or watching a woman grind mostly naked against a metal pole. Dino wasn't one of those men. Once he saw one or two strippers, he'd pretty much seen them all. It certainly didn't help that he saw them every night when he came into the club to do business.

"Three," Theo said.

Dino pushed his papers away, and grabbed the stacks of cash he'd set aside. Tying a rubber band around one of the smaller piles, he tossed it over to his brother. Theo caught it without hesitation, stuffing the rolled up bills into his pocket, his pay for the week.

"Vet them for me?" Dino asked. "I've got a headache and I need a drink."

Theo cocked an eyebrow. "You okay?"

That seemingly simple question took Dino off guard for a second, if only because his younger brother rarely put forth any effort to actually seem like he *cared*. Dino didn't mind because it was just Theo's personality. Some shit couldn't be helped. They were products of their violent raising.

Dino was the same way, mostly.

"Fine, just tired. Will you do it?"

Theo shrugged. "Do I have to act like I'm interested?"

"Are you?"

"Hardly."

"Then no, just vet them. I only need one to fill Chrissy's spot for the duration of her pregnancy. Make sure whichever one gets the job knows that once Chrissy decides to come back to work, their position will no longer be needed."

"Got it," Theo said over his shoulder, already leaving Dino behind.

Dino stared at his brother's back as Theo disappeared down the hallway.

Story of his life … He was always watching people walk away; he had yet to find a person he wanted to follow after.

"What'll it be, boss?"

Dino took a seat on the bar stool, waving at the many bottles behind the bartender. "Vodka, straight."

Tossing the bar rag over his shoulder, the man turned to ready Dino's drink. In less than a minute, Dino was sipping on the best vodka the club stocked, and the thumping in his temples began to lessen.

If only for a short while …

Out of the corner of his eye, Dino watched as Theo sat down in a private, roped off section of the club to do what he'd been asked.

It was only when he heard his brother call out a name, asking for the woman to come out from the back, did Dino really pay attention.

"Karen Martin, you're up first, sweetheart."

Dino blinked, his glass freezing as he tipped it up for another drink.

Karen.

He hadn't heard that name spoken once in how many months?

Three now, at least.

It had to be random, he thought. *Had to be.* There were more Karens in Chicago than the one Dino had met months ago, and purposely chose to ignore because she did nothing more than make him smile.

Besides, hadn't she said she was a photographer?

She was, and he knew she was.

He had no reason to get bothered and uncomfortable, simply because another woman shared the same name as her.

Except …

Dino's throat tightened, and he sat a little straighter on the barstool.

Except it *was* the same Karen he'd met all those months ago in the cemetery that walked out on the stage wearing a black lace ensemble that showed off just about *everything.* On their own accord, Dino's gaze traveled up the long length of tanned legs, the swell of hips, and a curve of a delicate waist. Slender fingers wrapped tightly around the metal pole when a song started up in the background, drawing Dino's attention to the black fingernail polish she wore.

Jesus.

Why was she here?

She was a photographer, not a stripper!

Better yet, why did it bother Dino so goddamn much?

He tried to ignore the scene happening twenty feet away, even going so far as turning his back to Karen and his brother, though he couldn't help but look over his shoulder every so often. To give Theo his due, he didn't seem all that interested in what was happening on the stage, only jotting down a note once in a while on the pad of paper in front of him on the table.

Before Dino knew it, he'd been staring at Karen for …

minutes.

Guessing by the time left in the song, she had another minute to go.

He could fix this situation fast enough if he really wanted to. Once she was done, he could remove her presence—and whatever strange interest he had in her—by simply telling his brother the first dancer was a no, and to choose between the following two. He could do it without Karen even seeing him, or knowing he was the one who owned the joint.

Dino didn't need to be getting himself involved with *people.*

He didn't need to be feeding interests that would lead nowhere.

What interest, his mind taunted, *she made you* smile.

Exactly.

It was nothing, and he wasn't going to make nothing into *something.*

Stupid people did dumb shit like that.

Dino was not stupid.

Then, he made the mistake of looking around, gaging patrons in the room. The club, when hiring dancers, always did the vetting when the place was open for business. That way, instead of simply judging the girls' ability to dance by what they could do on the pole, they could also take note of which dancer the male patrons seemed to pay more attention to.

There were a lot of eyes on Karen.

More than Dino was comfortable with.

Hot in his gut, he clenched his hand tighter around the glass, trying to ignore the strange sensations coursing through his nervous system. He didn't know the woman, nothing beyond her name and *one* of her professions. They'd never even had a half-decent conversation. Where in the fuck did he get off *feeling* like he had any say over what she did or who looked at her?

Apparently, it didn't matter.

Or rather, Dino's body decided it didn't matter for him.

He was getting up off his chair when he knew there was perhaps another thirty seconds left to the song. The beautiful woman spinning around on the pole in six-inch black heels didn't seem to notice as Dino approached Theo from behind, though that could be because of the shadows in the club.

All too soon, Dino was at his brother's back and tapping

Theo on the shoulder.

"What—"

"Move," Dino ordered.

Theo turned in the chair completely, giving his brother a strange look. "I'm doing what you told me to."

"And now you're moving."

With a frustrated sigh, Theo tossed his pen down, got up, and headed for the bar. It was only when Dino sat down in the leather chair his brother had vacated did the woman dancing with nothing but scraps of lace to cover her body finally notice him.

Karen damn near stumbled in her heels as her gaze landed on Dino.

He was pretty sure he was a sight to see for her.

He knew how he looked on a regular basis—cold featured, well-dressed, and unapproachable.

He was all of that in those moments, except he was more then, too. More, because his gaze was locked on her, his pants were getting uncomfortable as fuck, and he was two seconds away from yanking her off that goddamn stage and covering her with his blazer.

Karen's mouth opened to speak, her grip on the pole tightening. "Dino—"

"Get down right now," Dino uttered.

The words had come out on their own accord, practically ripping from his chest and forcing their way past his clenched teeth.

Karen's eyes widened. "What?"

"Get down before I bring you down myself."

He wasn't very good at the whole communication thing.

He figured he was clear enough, because Karen didn't hesitate to listen.

The moment Karen's heels clicked on the hardwood floor of the club, Dino was standing, shrugging his coat off and tossing it over her shoulders. She didn't refuse the jacket, her gaze drawn down to the floor as he began directing her toward the back offices.

"What are you doing?" Karen asked.

Dino scoffed.

He didn't have a fucking clue.

"I could ask you the same thing."

"Trying to get a *job*," Karen said quietly.

Dino could hear the slightest hint of shame in her voice, like that statement was the very last thing she wanted to admit, especially to him.

As soon as Dino got Karen through the threshold of his office, and slammed the door closed, she jerked out of his hold and spun on her sky-high heels. The click-clack of them hitting the floor drew his attention down to her long-as-fuck legs.

Again.

Get out of your head!

Or rather, he needed to stop thinking with his cock.

At that thought, Dino shifted his gaze to Karen's face, doing all he could to ignore the way her cheeks were the sweetest color of pink, and how much his fucking cock liked the look of her embarrassment.

"I can walk just fine, thank you," Karen said, shrugging Dino's jacket of her shoulders and handing it over to him. "And I came here to dance, not to be covered up. What is your problem?"

She had no way of knowing this strip club belonged to Dino, of that, he was most sure. He'd only recently gotten it from Ben, as far as that went, and beyond that, he had never given Karen his last name during their two previous meetings.

This was all … random.

Or fate, his mind taunted further.

Right, fate.

Dino didn't believe in coincidences, but he also didn't believe in shit like destiny, either.

"I thought you were a photographer," Dino said, his words coming out almost accusatory.

"I am. I also need to pay my bills, thanks."

Ouch.

The bite in her tone stung.

"And who the hell are you to pull me down off the stage like that?" Karen asked when Dino stayed silent.

"The asshole that owns the place."

Karen's fight deflated in an instant. "Oh."

Dino's guilt climbed higher—he didn't believe Karen had done anything wrong, or had anything to be ashamed of, but he was clearly making her feel that way.

Clearing his throat and glancing away, Dino dared to ask,

"You seemed very … well-versed on the stage."

"Is that your way of asking me if I strip often?"

"No, that's—"

"I went to art school for photography and dance. I could only make a career out of one of them after I broke my knee climbing the side of a bridge to get a shot of a river. But even that's crapping out considering I am one of *hundreds* of photographers in this goddamn city that's struggling to make ends meet."

Well, then …

"Okay," Dino said, giving Karen his attention again.

She cocked a brow at him. "Okay? Does that mean you're going to move so I can go out and finish what I was doing?"

"No."

"No?"

Dino shook his head. "Nope."

No way in hell.

CHAPTER 5

"YOU need a job, I'll get you a job."

Those words were haunting Dino. If only because he'd done exactly what he said for Karen, and got her set up in his restaurant working as a server. But because he couldn't just leave it at that, and had checked up on her several times over the period of a couple of weeks, he'd quickly learned he was undervaluing her ability and what she was capable of. The woman had a knack for numbers and schedules, something that particular restaurant had trouble with since opening.

It seemed like they were always short on staff because of scheduling issues, and the books were a mess because like most of his businesses that were able to hide funds, Dino shoved dirty money into the records to hide it from the government. But he didn't want the bookkeeper to *know* he was doing it, and so, expected them to show where it was coming from without *showing* where it was actually coming from.

Now, at a month and a half after she walked into his strip club, the woman was scheduling his employees, working the books like a pro, and seemed quite happy doing it.

Dino shouldn't *know* how well she was doing at all, never mind that she was happy about it, but he did.

He made at least two trips a week to a restaurant he had previously despised visiting just to see Karen. She never asked him why he showed up at random times with a coffee in hand for her, simply took it with a smile and continued working on whatever task she had for the day.

Today was no exception.

Dino pretended to flip through a recent order of supplies while Karen typed away on the laptop, muttering under her breath every so often about extra cash and where it came from.

He hid his smirk by looking down.

She had to know—like his previous bookkeeper—that he was pillowing funds into the business. She had to realize she was, essentially, cooking his books to make it all look on the up and up.

Karen never said a thing.

"So …"

Dino glanced up at Karen's random statement. She was staring right at him, those soul-deep brown eyes of hers lighting up with curiosity. Her pretty features distracted him for a moment, keeping him from responding as he took in full lips and flushed cream skin. It never failed to amaze him how she always looked as though the whole world—everything surrounding her—interested her with all its details, even the mundane things.

It shocked him that she seemed interested in him at all.

She was friendly like that, where he simply … well, wasn't.

"Yes?" Dino asked.

"When are you going to gain the courage to speak up?"

Dino shifted a bit in the chair, confused. "I beg your pardon?"

Karen smiled, shaking her head and going back to her work on the laptop. "Never mind, Dino."

He was lost.

"I mean," she continued, never looking up from the laptop again, "we can keep doing this, if it's what you like. You coming here, me pretending like I don't know what you're up to."

"Again—what?"

"Just ask, Dino," Karen said, shooting him with a look that pinned him to the chair.

Dino laughed. "Why don't you tell me what you want me to ask, and then we'll go from there?"

Karen's fingers stopping moving on the keyboard. "So you're telling me there's no particular reason why you show up here to check up on the place, yet you only ever really seem to stick around me, with a coffee *for* me, and there's *no* reason for you doing that?"

Well …

Dino felt his smile growing, and he couldn't have stopped it if he tried. Karen wasn't a stupid woman—he'd learned that quickly, which was why instead of serving people food and drinks, she was sitting behind a desk in her very own office, with a brand new laptop to do her work on. He certainly didn't think his interest in her was going unnoticed, but he *had* hoped she wouldn't look too deep into it.

Truth was, Dino didn't know what to do about how he felt.

Having interest and attraction was one thing.

Acting on it was something else entirely.

Dino hadn't had a *thing* with a woman in years, and the last one he had ended in a way that still kept him up at night. He hadn't loved the woman, but he felt responsible for the hell that had come down upon her simply because she had been with him.

And that, in a nutshell, had been more than enough to keep him wary of any other relationship. He couldn't give a woman normal things—not a home, a family, and a stable life. He wasn't of the right mindset to do those sorts of things.

"Dino?" Karen asked, bringing him from his thoughts.

He looked to her again, taking in her soft smile that always got a little bigger when she graced him with it. "Yeah?"

"Just *ask*."

Dino just stared at Karen, unsure if he should act on his strange attraction, or leave it be. She didn't know a lot about him, or his life. She didn't have a clue about the things he was involved in, or the family he came from.

She never asked.

He never offered.

Then, Dino had to consider other things, too. Or rather, people.

Like Ben DeLuca.

A man so determined to control the people who shared his last name that he would go as far as hurting those same people just to gain what he wanted from them.

Dino was not an exception to that rule—Ben practically broke the rule in on Dino's fucking back.

Ben would never approve of someone like Karen. A non-Italian, an outsider to their family and the lifestyle they lived, someone from a lower economic status with nothing to bring to the Outfit.

When Ben didn't approve … horrible things happened.

That was enough to cement Dino's next decision.

"There's nothing to ask," Dino said, getting up from his chair and tossing the paperwork to the desk. "Have a great evening, and let me know if you need anything or something needs looked over again."

Karen's smile faded slightly.

It hurt him to see her dejected expression.

So he made sure not to look back at her as he left the office.

It was for the best, he told himself.

He couldn't start *something* with someone.

It would only end in pain.

Nighttime was the worst for Dino.

The darkness brought back rushes of memories he would rather forget in the form of nightmares that he couldn't escape.

He did well in the day, for the most part, to ignore his simmering anxiety and the pressure constantly building in his chest. He put on a good act with his suits hiding scars and his sunglasses hiding tired, worn eyes.

But at night, when he was alone, there was no way to hide.

His way to combat the need to sleep was to work.

Constant movement helped. So did working out, though sometimes that worked against him and made him even more tired.

Dino could spend hours cleaning guns, or his apartment, and he'd once spent an entire night reorganizing his collection of old books, simply because he'd expended his effort on every other thing and there was nothing else to *do*.

He'd become a pro at ignoring sleep at night.

Sleeping in the day was slightly easier, and he was less likely to dream when he took a quick hour-long nap on an uncomfortable couch or in the driver's seat of his car.

Sometimes, though, his days were too busy and he just couldn't get those hour or two naps in between whatever he had to do.

Those were the worst.

One day led into two, and then three.

The longest he'd gone without sleep was four and a half days.

The night that followed had, quite literally, left him stuck in nightmares he couldn't wake from for hours.

It was in those nightmares that he relived pain.

Beatings.

Bleeding.

Dark basements.

Damp floors.

Vomit.

Pain.

Ben DeLuca had made it his mission to mold his nephews into the creatures he wanted them to be—into perfect, unfeeling soldiers he could use—after they were left orphans with no parents. The first time it happened was on the night Ben had killed Dino's parents, and that beating left him damn near dead, and then recovering for a week in the locked basement of one of Ben's many shoddy, abandoned rental properties.

It didn't stop with just one.

No, at any slight, at even the smallest of offense to Ben's mind, a punishment would follow. If for any reason, Dino didn't do what his uncle wanted, if he didn't behave the way Ben deemed he should or anything of a similar sort, he would quickly find himself bleeding and healing in a place where his pleads for help couldn't—or wouldn't—be heard.

Sometimes Dino had fought back, but it was only after Ben's awful attention fell more prominently to a young Theo, did he stop.

He never wanted his brother to experience the hell he did where their uncle was concerned.

Or, God forbid, their little sister Lily.

So he kept Ben's attention on him through his later teenaged years and into his twenties. He made Ben focus on *his* fuckups, instead of Theo's.

Well, as much as he could.

Sometimes he failed.

Those memories were the worst—the ones where he knew he hadn't been good enough, or strong enough, to protect his brother.

It was really no wonder why Theo didn't particularly like

Dino.

Weakness came in many forms.

Dino had too many to name.

Perhaps that was why, when Dino was working on his third night of no sleep with little to no naps in the daytime, he found himself in a place where sleeping could very well be at the cost of his life.

Strolling into what looked to be an abandoned warehouse in the shipping district of Chicago, Dino was instantly alert at the sound of shouts—both excited and filled with pain. He paid the over-hanging, blinking lights very little attention as he followed the sounds of fighting down the long hallway. At the end, enforcers blocked the entrance, waiting for payment to move aside, though at the sight of him, they both moved anyway.

Underground fighting was a dangerous game.

There were no losers, per say, only dead bodies to dispose of.

And yet, while the violence wasn't something Dino particularly enjoyed getting involved in hands-on, he did own the warehouse, and by providing the place, he earned himself an income. The fights were invite-only, and on a need-to-know basis.

That way, those who came in were known to only a few people who regularly attended or fought. The money was damn good, both for Dino, and the winners.

Finding a spot against the wall so that he could watch the two fighters beating the hell out of one another in the makeshift ring, Dino's anxiety began to settle. It helped when there were people watching, because that forced him to make sure no one knew he had a constant war going on in his mind.

A war that was killing him slowly.

It was only when a form settled beside him on the wall did Dino finally look away from the fight.

"How've you been, Ghost?" Dino asked.

Damian Rossi—a long-time friend of Dino's younger brother—shrugged his shoulders. "Busy."

"That's a good thing, though."

"Maybe."

Damian was a man of few words, and that worked well to his favor. After all, he hadn't gained his nickname for nothing, and the man could blend into a crowd like nobody Dino had ever met before. Involved in the Rossi faction of the Outfit, Damian worked as both an enforcer, and a personal hitman to the boss, Terrance.

Though if truth be told, Damian was any man's hitman.

For the right price.

Dino knew when it came right down to it, Damian only did what *he* wanted to do where the Outfit and jobs were concerned. He certainly made it seem like he and his set of skills were up for purchase, but Dino had also known Damian to decline more often than he accepted.

"What brings you around?" Dino asked.

Damian tilted his head to the side, his gaze sweeping the floor and the people. "Checking things out, man."

That didn't sound right.

"Why?"

"You're paying dues on this place, right?" Damian asked instead of answering.

Now, Dino was really getting irritated.

"Why wouldn't I pay dues to the boss, Damian?"

Damian didn't answer right away, simply put his back to the wall and let out a sigh. "Ben has been around Terrance a lot lately, saying shit about the Capos doing work on the side and keeping dues that are owed from the boss."

Jesus.

Was that Ben's new plan? Get Terrance all worked up about his men and looking into their business until he caused a fucking problem that would start up another fucking feud?

Dino was not in the mood for that mess.

"I pay my dues," Dino said. "Pass the fucking message along, Ghost."

Damian nodded once, then pushed off the wall. "Never thought you didn't, Dino. Say hello to Theo for me."

"Do it yourself the next time you see him."

"He's in a mood lately. By the way, how's your sister? I heard she went to Europe a while back."

Dino didn't answer Damian's question.

He was already walking away himself.

CHAPTER
6

"OKAY, at first I thought maybe it was just me making shit up, but now I *know* you're avoiding me."

Dino stiffened at Karen's accusatory words, cursing silently that he hadn't just come when the restaurant was closed, and not a day that she was supposed to have off. He'd avoided her for two weeks by staying away from the business, but today he hadn't been given much of a choice when he needed to go over paperwork for an order that was missing several items. He'd called ahead of time, learning that Karen was off for the day, and decided to make his way in.

But apparently she wasn't off.

"Thought you were off today," Dino said, never turning away from his work.

Karen scoffed. "You're not even going to deny it, then?"

"There's nothing to deny."

"*Right.*"

He could hear the sarcasm thick in her tone, but there was something else, too.

Hurt, maybe.

Dino couldn't dwell on it for long, or he'd find regrets in his behavior. He wasn't the type to get caught up in his feelings—he didn't have the time for nonsense of that sort.

"Something you need?" Dino asked.

"Actually, yes."

"And that is what, exactly?"

"You."

Dino damn near choked on air, surprised at her blatant statement. He turned fast to face her, only to find her smiling at him in a way that said she'd caught him somehow.

"Say that again, Karen."

"You asked if there was something I needed."

"Yes," Dino said, "keep going."

"I need you to stop avoiding me like I did something wrong. And if I did do something wrong, the very least you could do is *tell me* what it fucking is."

Karen rarely swore. The first time they met, he remembered her using a cuss, and thinking it was probably a regular thing, except it wasn't. That had been nothing more than a fluke. In all the time Dino had spent with her since she started working for him, he could count on one hand the amount of cusses she let slip past her pretty lips.

He didn't even think the F-word was in her vocabulary.

How mistaken he was ...

"You didn't do anything wrong," Dino settled on saying.

He couldn't give her much more.

"But you *are* avoiding me," she pressed.

God.

She was not going to let this go.

"I'm avoiding an awkward situation," Dino replied, adding, "which you're not helping with at the moment."

"Because I wanted you to take me on a *date?*"

Dino blinked. "What?"

Karen looked as though she had taken all she could for the day. Throwing her hands up, she let out an exhausted noise and spun on her heel to leave.

Dino couldn't let her go like that. In a blink, he was going after her, catching up with her in the hallway. He grabbed her arm, spinning her around to face him.

"Wait a second," he said.

Karen's scowl cut him deep and she jerked out of his hold. "Don't manhandle me, Dino. I'm not a pet for you to play with, you know?"

Dino dropped her arm, taking one giant step back. "Sorry."

"Listen, if you're not interested in me, then that's fine. But the signals you are throwing out are a little mixed, all right? One second you're watching me like you can't get enough, the next you're turning into a block of ice. So I took a risk and asked you, just so I knew. I don't mind rejection, asshole, but you don't need to make it more painful than it already is. If you're *not* interested, then say so. Don't be a dick about it, too."

Well, then.

Dino wasn't quite sure what to say.

"I'm … *very* interested," he managed to utter.

It took a lot for him to say that.

If he wanted a girl to climb in bed with, he could go find one at a club, and he wouldn't even need to waste his breath learning her name before he was done with her.

Karen wasn't quite the same.

He actually found himself genuinely *curious* about her—who she was, where she came from, and why she painted her fingernails black when she wore the brightest colors everywhere else. He wasn't looking to get his dick wet—though he'd be lying if he said his cock wasn't interested in Karen—but rather, he wanted to know her.

That couldn't end well.

He hadn't done this sort of thing before.

Karen shifted in her heels, watching him out of the corner of her eyes. "Oh?"

Dino nodded. "I'm not very good at this, I guess."

That was an understatement.

He didn't get *involved* with people at all.

"It's just a date," she said softly.

"That's not so bad," Dino replied, "but I'm not sure I can give you much beyond that, Karen."

"Did I ask for more?"

"No."

"Then don't put words in my mouth," Karen said, smirking just a bit. "You're a little strange, Dino DeLuca."

He didn't miss how she said his last name like she had no fucking clue how dangerous that surname was—as if she didn't possibly know the ties his name had to organized crime and a hellish past that was still very much alive and well in Chicago.

She didn't have a clue.

That, or she didn't care.

"Ask me," Karen said.

Dino chuckled. "My last date was years ago."

Ten years, to be exact.

He'd watched his date be buried a week later.

Ben hadn't *approved.*

Terrance never knew what really happened to his daughter.

Didn't Dino have a good reason to be wary?

"Ask me," she repeated.

Dino shouldn't—he knew better.

He still did it.

It had been a *long* time since he'd done something that he wanted to do.

"Drinks or coffee?" he asked.

Karen smiled, warm and wide. "Let's get drinks, and if goes well ..."

"What?"

"We might end up with coffee, too."

Damn.

Dino had learned things about Karen over the two months since she had started working at his restaurant—she was only a year younger than him, and she'd moved from California to Chicago for school, decided she'd liked it, and then stayed after graduation. But those were safe things; the surface of a tale, and not the whole story.

It was only after her third beer in a quiet bar did he start to learn the good stuff.

"My mother and father separated when I was thirteen," Karen said, working on peeling the label off the beer bottle. "I didn't spend much time with my dad, but he thought he had enough say to tell me Chicago was a terrible choice and I would be stupid to leave home."

"Yet here you are," Dino said.

Karen giggled, tipping up her bottle for another drink. "Here I am."

"Do you miss home?"

"Miss the sun and the beaches," she offered. "Sometimes. I like the snow."

"I'm sure that makes up for it."

Karen shrugged. "Does for me. Snow makes for beautiful pictures."

He wondered just how much time she was able to devote to photography given she spent five days a week at his restaurant working eight-hour days. She was paid well, which he was sure she appreciated, but it wasn't her passion.

Artists thrived on passion.

"And what do your parents think now?" Dino asked.

Karen's brow furrowed. "About me being in Chicago?"

"Yeah."

"Well, I don't know. I haven't talked to them in about a year now. I haven't gone back for a visit because …" She trailed off, a sweet pink coloring her cheeks. "I just haven't gone back."

"Because you couldn't afford to?" Dino asked.

Karen glanced away, taking in the quiet people milling about in the bar and enjoying their evening. He'd allowed her to pick the place, if only because the establishments he would go to would probably be mob connected and his main goal in whatever he was doing with her was to keep her far away from that mess. She didn't need to be involved in that side of his life, even if her only involvement would be through him.

"Yeah, that's … accurate."

"Do they know that's why you haven't been back?" he asked.

Karen laughed, but this time it was bitter and sad. "Why would I tell them that? So they can say they were right—this whole plan of mine was a major fuck up and look at how spectacularly I failed at it?"

Ouch.

"You're not failing, Karen. I know failure—this isn't it."

"Oh?"

Just like that, Dino felt the proverbial table turn to him.

He'd been careful throughout the date, only letting her chat about what she wanted, and doing his best to deflect any questions about his history or life without making it extremely obvious that's what he was actually doing. She didn't seem to mind that he didn't want to go too in depth with his own stories, and she enjoyed talking.

Frankly, he *really* enjoyed listening to her.

It'd been a long time since he just talked to someone.

Since he enjoyed the company of others.

Too long, maybe.

"You know, I can see it when you sort of blink out on me, Dino," Karen said.

Dino cleared his throat, setting his bottle of beer on the bar. "I'm not sure what you mean."

"You often go inside your head. It makes me wonder what's so interesting in there that it's where you want to be."

"My head is not an interesting place, believe me."

A war zone, maybe.

Hell, likely.

Certainly not *interesting*.

"I don't believe that for a second," Karen said quietly. "I went back to your mother's grave for a couple of weeks after you stopped coming on Sundays—just to say hello to her, and wipe down the stone. I figured if you had done it for so long, maybe it was difficult for you to just up and stop simply because you had to in order to avoid me."

"I wasn't—"

"Are we going back to that again?"

Dino let out a laugh at her pointed glare. She was right, and rightly called him out on the lie. But the laugh ... that was what surprised him the most. It was genuine, and deep. It almost made his stomach ache, though it didn't last long and was over before he realized.

Sad thing was, it was not the *first* time or even the second time that she had made him laugh without even trying.

It was all a little surreal.

Who was this woman?

Why *her*, he found himself wondering.

"Dino," Karen whispered, drawing him from his thoughts.

It was something else a little strange about her—he always found he liked being *outside* of his head when he was with her, rather than inside where he could ignore the world, even if his mind was full of terrible things.

"Yeah?" he asked, watching her more intently than before.

"You've been staring at my mouth for the last five minutes."

Had he?

Well, she *had* been talking.

It certainly wasn't because a part of his mind wondered what her lips felt like, and another part of his brain was curious what she tasted like and how she kissed.

Dino had spent so long keeping his emotions shut off from the rest of the world, because it was easier to deal with life when he didn't have the complication of feeling to go along with it, and he didn't quite know how to discern the things he felt *now*. Making sure he never got involved with people meant he didn't need to put forth a great deal of effort to understand them or why they did the things they did.

Karen made him want to know all of those things, especially why she made him *want* it.

It felt like he was playing with fire.

She was right.

He *was* a little strange.

"Dino," Karen said, laughing low.

"Just ask, right?"

Karen nodded, her grin deepening. "Right."

He was caught staring at her mouth again, and how her lips curved upwards at the edges whenever she glanced his way.

Just ask.

"I'd like to kiss you," he admitted.

"I didn't hear a question there."

"It's self-explanatory."

"I did say coffee was a possibility," Karen mused.

"I'm only asking for a kiss."

"We both know it's not going to end at a kiss, Dino."

Even as he leaned forward, closing the distance between them to catch her smiling lips with his own, he knew she was right.

It wasn't the first time she had been, and he doubted it would be the last.

All those thoughts drifted away, and his mind quieted, as he felt her lips move against his. Soft and steady, slow and sweet.

It still burned him all over.

Suddenly, he was reminded what it felt like to be alive.

All because of a kiss.

CHAPTER
7

KAREN had been right—*entirely* so.

One kiss was not enough once Dino had been given it. One kiss turned into two, and then three. Before he knew what had happened, he'd pulled her from the barstool and onto his lap where he could finish his beer while his hand grabbed tightly to her inner thigh under the skirt of her dress.

He thought they'd make their way to her place, maybe.

His was too far away.

A hotel for the night would work just fine, too.

Shit.

They didn't make it past the parking lot.

Dino fell into the backseat of his car with a chuckle as Karen climbed into his lap and straddled his waist. With the door closed, the windows tinted dark, and the corner of the parking lot hidden in the shadows, he couldn't find a single reason *why not*.

That was just fine for him.

The backseat wasn't very big, and he didn't have a great deal of room to move. Those reasons made his first few moves hesitant and stilted when he reached for Karen.

Or maybe it was because it'd been a while since he'd been in this situation.

Dino had plenty of opportunities for sex if he wanted it, and on the occasions when he felt the need, he acted on it and that was it. He rarely even asked those women's names; he went into it with zero expectations, and so did his partner for the night.

Karen was not the same.

Not at all.

She also wasn't having his hesitance.

"Dino," Karen said, shifting on his lap in such a way that damn near made him groan. "Don't think about this too much right now."

"I can do that."

He was sure he could.

He could feel the soft cotton between her thighs, warm and thin. Her core grinded down on the hard length of his erection. Her hands found his face, and she made him look at her. She clouded his vision—pretty brown eyes and pouty pink lips. And then in a blink, those lips of hers were on his, moving and melding, parting just enough to let his tongue snake in to find that taste and heat that he'd wondered about earlier.

It was as good as he expected, if not better.

Karen's thighs tightened just a bit to Dino's waist, and her fingernails dragged over the scruff on his jaw when she tilted her head back, giving him access to the delicate column of her throat. It was the slight bite of pain from her touch, followed by the happiest, quiet sigh she released, that did it for him.

The small amount of anxiety he'd been feeling drifted away.

The control he was keeping was gone.

The desire to feel something other than a black nothingness beat deep in his blood, thumping harder with every beat of his heart. It was so unusual for him to get to the point he currently was when he *did* find himself in the midst of a hookup—fisting her clothes and yanking them off to get *more* skin and *more* to feel and taste.

But he wanted that with Karen. Wanted to see her skin and find out if his hands fit into her curves, and *God*, maybe he could get her to give him another one of those sighs.

It wasn't long at all before Karen was exactly how Dino wanted her, naked, in his lap, and free for him to explore. Every swipe of his thumbs over pebbling skin earned him the sweetest sounds. The slide of his hands up her throat and his fingers curling around her neck made her breath hitch and her lashes flutter when her eyes closed.

Yet, it was between her thighs where he wanted to be the most. He kept his hand on her throat, feeling his fingers tangle into strands of her hair and his other hand slipped lower. A shiver worked its way through Karen's body, from her legs to her shoulders, when he finally got his hand on her sex. A hot wetness met the tips of his fingers, the softness of her sex pushing down into his hand to find more.

She wasn't shy, he found.

Not when two of his fingers thrust in, and she didn't hold back from reaching down to hold his wrist in place, keeping him like he was for a second.

He didn't mind at all.

His thumb came up to slide along the hood of her clit, and Dino's gaze flew up to find Karen watching him with parted lips and anticipation shining brightly.

He bet she was beautiful when she came.

In that moment, that was all he really wanted to see.

"Come—let me have it," Dino said, surprised at the hoarseness of his words.

His demand was punctuated by another thrust of his fingers and the circle of his thumb over her throbbing clit. Under his touch, she trembled, her hips meeting his hand and her lip finding its way between her teeth as the walls of her sex hugged his digits tighter.

Dino quickly realized this was going to be an addicting sight for him—having her like this, watching her so caught up in it all.

He wasn't ready to think on it for long, but he *liked* it.

"*Shit*," Karen breathed.

Her soft exclamation was followed by another round of tremors crawling over her body as her pussy contracted hard around his fingers. His name fell from her mouth, loud and lovely, as she came.

Dino had been right. She was beautiful when she came.

Flushed, lost, and free.

Very few things compared, he thought.

It was only after she'd calmed did he withdraw from her body, going in search of a condom packet he knew should be in his dash. Karen's fingers trailed over his neck as he leaned between the seats, quickly finding the condom before he fell into the back with her once more.

He wasted no time then, kissing her hard and deep while her fingers worked the buttons on his shirt open and he got his pants undone just enough to reach in for his cock. Karen only broke away long enough to grab the condom from his hold, open the foil packet, and then fit the latex down his length before her mouth was back on his.

The softness and heat of her mouth warring with his damn near matched the satiny warmth of her pussy as she grinded over him again. Dino had no time for teasing, his interest in that had waned the moment she'd come on his hand.

Grabbing her waist tightly, Dino lifted Karen just enough to get her positioned where she needed to be, and then he was pulling her down. The move was hard—fast—but she didn't seem to mind. As he slid into her clenching sex with the one thrust, her head fell back and caramel-toned waves of her hair tumbled over her shoulders.

"Jesus, yeah," Karen mumbled.

Dino could only moan his approval in response.

She was snug all around him—slick and contracting in all the right places. His heart raced as she lifted and lowered on him all over again, making his lungs ache with his next exhale.

He was more than willing to let her control the pace, if only because he couldn't think beyond the scent of sex in the car and the beautiful creature working her body above his.

"There, Jesus, yeah ... right there," Karen said, her teeth catching her bottom lip.

Dino kissed the reddened, plump flesh when she let her bite go. "Fucking *beautiful.*"

He wasn't a big talker to begin with, and he was even less inclined to talk during sex.

But he couldn't help but tell her how she looked.

That he wanted her sounds.

That she felt *so fucking good.*

It took only a few jerky thrusts after Karen had come a second time for Dino to follow, the sensations coursing from his balls to his spine as he emptied into latex.

He wanted more of *her* the second he was done.

"Two coffees," Dino said, putting in his order.

Karen piped up as his hand pressed to her lower back. "Two sugar, three cream in mine, please."

"Black for the other."

The barista nodded her head, already turning to make the order.

"Oh, and two cherry cheese Danishes," Karen added.

"Working on giving me diabetes," Dino muttered.

Karen grinned widely. "Don't pretend like you don't have a sweet tooth, Dino. I remember the donuts and cakes you brought in with my coffees, thank you."

She had him there.

"And two Danishes," Dino told the barista.

There was no point in arguing with Karen.

Besides, he was fucking starved. He'd spent the night—happily—with Karen at his side. Driving around Chicago, talking because it felt good and he liked listening to her talk, but also because he wasn't quite ready for it to end.

He only realized it was morning when the sun finally started coming up.

It was crazy.

Perfect, but crazy.

"Thank you," Karen said, bringing Dino from his thoughts.

Their order was ready, waiting on the counter.

How easy it was for him to lose track of time around Karen.

Even if it was *only* minutes.

"I never said it last night, but thank you," Dino said once he had coffee in his hands and his back was turned to the barista working the counter. "I appreciate it."

Karen blinked up at him, smiling in the strangest way. Her shoulders lifted under his blazer, as she hadn't brought a coat with her and he didn't want to see her be cold. She almost seemed to be swallowed by his jacket, and it was only then that he realized how small she looked next to him.

He liked that a bit too much. In a way, she was perfectly safe with him. She certainly looked happy to be tucked into his side like she was.

"You're thanking me," Karen replied as they slipped into a booth side by side. "For what, screwing you in the backseat of a car?"

The laughter that broke free from Dino's chest was almost foreign to him, as he hadn't laughed that hard in a long while, and it felt both good and strange. Actually, he had laughed that hard recently—the night before with Karen. It was with *her* that he felt … different; that he felt okay to laugh.

Karen handed over the Danish sweets she'd been holding, her smile growing. "You're very handsome when you laugh, Dino."

Well, he hadn't been expecting *that*.

"I don't do it very often," he admitted.

"You should do it more."

With her, he doubted she would give him much of a choice in that matter.

He didn't mind all that much.

Sipping from her coffee, Karen moved closer into his side, letting him wrap an arm around her waist. It was difficult to ignore how his laughter had gained the attention of several people in the small coffee shop, but it was made easier by having her close.

He could focus on her, not them.

Dino's whole life had been an attempt to stay *out* of the limelight.

"Not for *last night*," Dino said, chuckling quietly.

"But we're definitely going to be working on a repeat." Karen winked up at him as her lips curved into a sensual smile around the rim of her coffee cup. "Right?"

How was he supposed to say no?

"Hell yeah."

Karen nudged him with her arm. "Go on—you're *thanking* me."

"Yes." Dino cleared his throat, feeling awkward for the first time since they'd fixed themselves up and climbed back into the front seat of his car. "For my mother's grave. You said you went back, and thank you for that."

Her gaze lowered, smile fading. "I intruded on something for you. I felt bad that you didn't want to come back."

"That was the problem," Dino muttered.

"What?"

"The problem—I *did* want to come back. I *did* hope you would be there."

Karen's brow furrowed. "But you didn't."

"I didn't," he echoed.

Karen didn't press him for *why*.

Dino was grateful.

He wasn't sure that he could properly explain it if she did ask, or if she would even understand.

It reminded him all over again that his life was a complete mess.

Dino had no idea what he was even doing being there with Karen.

Except he liked it.

So he knew damn well that it wasn't going to end anytime soon.

CHAPTER 8

CHINESE. My place. Tonight.

Three sentences.

Four simple words.

Nothing had ever sounded better.

Dino texted Karen back a quick confirmation, his attention stuck firmly on his phone instead of the meeting at hand. All he had to do was drop off his dues for the past month and then he could go, so it wasn't like his attention was currently needed.

Men chatted all around him, discussing issues that had come up over the last month and ventures they were currently pursing. It was, usually, one of the few times Dino cared to jump into conversation with the Capos and upper bosses of the Outfit, if only because it meant money, and he liked making money.

But … Karen.

Another text came in, making his phone vibrate in his hand and snagging his attention once more.

Grab me a bottle of wine?

Dino smiled, amused. She did like her wine, especially after working all day.

Sure, he texted back.

And chocolate. Definitely chocolate, too.

Chuckling low, Dino texted back a confirmative answer on that request, too.

It'd been a month since that night in the back of his car—*many* times followed that one, though Dino usually went back to that one because that was where it all started. And wasn't the beginning of something always the best?

He thought so.

Karen's involvement in the personal side of his life was like a breath of fresh air. He often found himself looking forward to their quiet nights, laughing over dinner or staying up way too late in her bed. It was simple, and simple things were the best kind of things to Dino. His life very rarely offered simple moments to make time actually seem like it was passing him by.

For the most part, his days were black, filled with people he didn't care about with demands and problems he couldn't give a shit for, making requests of him that he didn't want to fill, but had no choice in the matter.

Karen was not the same.

She was a small bit of light in his dismal life. Someone he didn't have to share with others because she had no idea about just how thinly strung Dino really was. She just enjoyed him, and the time he was able to give.

There were no rules or labels put on whatever relationship he had with Karen. She didn't expect things from him, or ask for more than he gave, for that matter. It made it easy—like breathing. He headed to her place three to four times a week, never bringing her to his because someone could show up at any time. She wasn't attached to the Outfit or its business, and he didn't think it was fair to involve her in it if only because she was involved with him.

That, and he wanted to keep her safe.

There were far too many people in the Outfit side of his life that would gladly use his involvement with an outsider to hurt him.

One, more so than others.

Speak of the devil …

Dino shoved his phone into his jacket pocket as Ben sat in a chair beside him in the restaurant. Ben never gave Dino an ounce of his attention as his gaze swept the many men waiting and chatting in the business. While it seemed like his uncle was entirely focused on the meeting at hand, Dino knew better. Ben was watching him—probably had been for a while—because he always did that shit.

"Do you have better things to be doing, other than playing on that phone of yours, Dino?" Ben asked.

Shit.

"Of course," Dino replied.

He was usually more careful where his attention was concerned, especially if it meant seeming distracted in front of his uncle. Ben was a shark—he'd latch onto any sign of weakness Dino had and history would repeat itself where he'd rip that chunk of weakness out, with no care of the harm or detriment it might cause.

Karen was not a weakness to Dino.

She was just a woman—one he found by chance and cared for if only because she made him happy.

It had been far too long since he had a small slice of happiness in his life.

He wasn't going to allow Ben DeLuca to take that happiness away from him.

"Well, you certainly seem ..."

Dino sighed inwardly, knowing it was coming.

"Distracted," Ben finished.

Yeah, there it was.

"One of my managers is having a problem with an employee. You know they defer to me on problems," Dino replied, wanting to keep Ben as far from his private, personal life as he could. He knew it was impossible, or rather, he wouldn't be able to keep Karen a secret forever. He was sure as hell going to try for as long as he could. "I'm here—where is Terrance?"

At his question about the Outfit boss's whereabouts, Ben seemed to accept the change in topic.

"On his way, Dino. He is on his way." Ben drummed his fingers to the table, peering across the room to where Theo sat at another table beside Damian Rossi. "Your brother is very cozy with the Rossi family."

Dino resisted the urge to roll his eyes. "He's *cozy* with no one but himself and whatever woman he's chosen to fuck for the weekend."

It was the best he could do for Theo. It may have come across as brash or rude, but it was true enough to keep Ben from Theo's personal life. What more could he ask for?

"You and I have different views of what being cozy means," Ben murmured, still watching Damian and Theo chat between one another.

"They've been friends since they were kids, Ben."

"I offered Damian a spot in the DeLuca family once."

Dino's brow rose at that statement. He, too, had a history

where Damian Rossi was concerned, though he doubted it was near the same as Ben's. A long time ago, when Damian was much younger and much more … volatile, Dino had hidden an incident caused by Damian that would have taken his life by the Outfit's rules. It was an easy choice to make, because he had been that age once, and he'd made mistakes. He knew Damian was a good kid after watching him with Theo and their younger sister Lily for a good many years when they were just young, for the most part, and so he did what he needed to do.

It left Damian with a debt of sorts.

Owed to Dino.

He would collect when he needed to.

"He refused me, of course," Ben said, still talking to himself. "I hadn't a need then to explain how wrong he was. I'm starting to regret that choice."

Dino's gaze flew back across to his brother and his friend.

Ben's statement could mean nothing good.

Not for Theo and certainly not for Damian.

It seemed innocent enough on the outside, a regret was what it was, but Ben rarely made those kind of statements without a follow-up that was almost always violent in nature, and left the victims bereft. History was a great predictor of future behavior.

Ben could not change his stripes overnight.

"Theo is too loose with his loyalties," Ben said.

"That's not true—he has a very small circle."

It just so happened that Damian was in that circle.

"Yes, but look at it this way, Dino. If it was you vying for the boss's seat, or Tommas Rossi, who would your brother choose to back? His *friend's* family, or the brother he can barely stand to talk to?"

Dino didn't care, but he was beginning to understand Ben's circle talk a bit better.

It left him feeling cold.

Should Ben decide to control whom Theo associated with outside of the DeLuca family, it would not end well for his younger brother. It also wouldn't end well for Damian.

Dino didn't want to see Theo or Damian in a pot of Ben's boiling water because his uncle was a fucking bastard.

It also didn't escape Dino's notice how Ben had once again mentioned someone in the DeLuca family taking the boss's seat, or *vying* for it, as he'd said. It might have only been in passing, but Ben was not the kind of man to make that statement without some kind of worth behind it. Perhaps that, more than anything else, was one of the most worrying things.

Dino didn't know where to focus first. He could only divert Ben's attention on so many things before he let others slip, or worse, Ben figured out what he was doing and came after Dino for fucking up whatever plans he may have.

Theo …

The Outfit …

Of course, Theo would always be infinitely more important than the Outfit to Dino. That was a no-brainer. It wasn't even a fucking question. Dino, no matter his brother's feelings about their shared past or the wounds between them that were not quite healed, would protect his brother at all costs. Even for something as simple as a *friendship* that was not approved by their uncle.

Blood before water, after all.

"… more important things," Ben said quietly.

Dino had only caught the tail end of Ben's sentence. "Pardon?"

Ben nodded toward Theo and Damian. "I will deal with that eventually, but at the moment, I have more important things to handle."

"Like what?"

Ben smiled, thin and cold. He stood from the table without a word, giving Dino a pat on the shoulder as he started his trek back to sit with the Outfit's front boss, Riley Conti. But over his shoulder, Dino heard his uncle's ending words.

"Be careful with your *distractions*, Dino."

Karen.

Suddenly, Dino had a heavy realization sink in.

He had three things to keep his uncle distracted from.

It wasn't *just* Theo and the Outfit.

It was Karen, too.

Or rather, Dino's involvement with Karen.

This was *exactly* why he didn't get mixed up in relationships or people.

It couldn't end well.

Glancing over his shoulder, Dino found that Ben was still watching him from across the restaurant. He felt his phone buzz in his pocket, and knew it was likely Karen messaging him again. He chose not to answer it, for his benefit, and hers.

He didn't think she would understand for a minute.

But he hoped it wouldn't hurt her too much.

Dino had to protect what he could, and Karen fell in line with that. It wasn't her fault she'd gotten mixed up with him, or the crazy, violent mess that was his life. She hadn't asked for anything more than a fun time with him.

She didn't ask for pain.

He had to try to keep her from the pain that was always a constant in his life in one way or another.

Almost all of it was caused by Ben.

So, when an hour had gone by, Terrance had finally arrived to accept his payments from his Capos, and then the men were dismissed, Dino went straight to his car, and then he went home. He didn't pick up that bottle of wine. He didn't go to Karen's place like he said he would.

She texted him later that night.

He read the incoming messages—one after the other.

Where are you?

Is everything okay?

You could answer me back, Dino.

Are you ignoring me now?

Each one became progressively more annoyed, and also worried. He could feel her concern, but also her anger, bleeding from every word.

Then, the final one came.

She didn't send another after that last one.

Fine. Whatever.

Dino didn't answer a single one back. He knew, for Karen's safety and to keep Ben from figuring out exactly where Dino's distractions were lately, he would need to stay away for a while.

That wouldn't bode well for him … or the relationship he had with Karen. She wouldn't understand why he was ignoring her. It wasn't really her fault, though. How could he expect her to understand?

He wouldn't be able to explain.

CHAPTER 9

"THIS is the biggest load of shit I have ever seen," Theo snarled.

Each and every word was thrown like daggers in Dino's direction. He was well aware that Theo was not pleased to be given yet another load of work, but it was what it was. Theo wouldn't care, nor would he understand, that his brother was keeping him busy in order to keep Ben's opinions of his personal business at a more pleasant level.

No, all Theo understood was Dino was unloading more responsibility onto his brother.

Including running the strip club.

Managing three more young guys in the crew.

Collecting payments on a schedule instead of having guys come to them.

They were little things, to be sure. It would all still add up and keep Theo working constantly on their side of Chicago. Damian, on the other hand, would be busy on his side of Chicago doing whatever his cousin and uncle needed of him for their family. It was a shitty way of going about it, but it would keep Ben from picking at Theo, or worse, really putting his hands into the friendship between the two young men to put a stop to it.

Of course, all Theo could see was Dino taking his own workload as a Capo, and tossing it onto his shoulders.

That was fine.

Dino could take Theo's anger. He could even roll with whatever idea Theo had about why Dino was doing all this so that his brother didn't know how truly awful their uncle was, and that Ben was up to his old tricks again.

Fact was, Theo, like Dino, still felt the aftereffects of growing up under Ben's violent hand. So his brother *did* know how terrible Ben could be, but there were still some games their uncle played that Dino wanted to keep Theo safe from.

It was better for everyone not to bring those memories to the surface.

Over the period of two weeks, since that day of the meeting, Dino had been very carefully adding one thing at a time to Theo's workload with their crew.

He had apparently met his limit.

"I've got a fucking *life*," Theo barked.

"So do I," Dino said absently, digging through the file cabinet.

He was missing paperwork, he was sure of it. Papers and information that came from offshore accounts, showing where his illegal funds were going and coming from. In order to know what he needed to hide, or rather, how *much* money he needed to hide, Dino needed those numbers.

He could always pull his records again, that wasn't the problem.

The problem was that he was positive he had put the records away, but they weren't where they should be.

"Right—a life," Theo said, his snarkiness growing. "Is that supposed to be a joke? It felt like a joke."

Dino sighed harshly, over the entire argument with his younger brother. "Listen, I am well aware you think I do nothing but sleep, eat, and breathe Outfit business, but the fact is, I do other shit, Theo. I have *other* interests. It's not going to hurt you to take on a bit more work for the crew, if nothing else, you might fucking learn something."

"Dino—"

"And isn't that the whole point? You want the title to go with the button—you're a made man, sure, but that means fuck all when you don't have the title, too. You want to be a Capo, little brother, put in the work for it."

Theo stewed in his anger, saying nothing in response.

Dino was grateful.

"Did you let someone in my office?" Dino asked as he flipped through the file for the fifth time.

"Who in the fuck would I let in your office?"

Dino stood straight, placing the file back in its spot and slamming the cabinet shut. He'd have to deal with the missing paperwork at another time. Maybe when he had an actual idea where the paper records might have gone.

"Nothing—never mind, it's not important," Dino said.

Theo stared hard at his brother as Dino grabbed his laptop off the desk, readying to leave. "Dino, I wouldn't let someone in here. You know that, right?"

He did.

Theo had just as much to lose as Dino did where the business was concerned, should certain records fall into the wrong hands. Besides that, the brothers also managed product out of the strip club at certain times during the month. The dealers came in, traded money for bricks of cocaine, and off they went to sell for the month.

Should the cops get wind of *any* of that business, they would be in a hell of a lot of trouble.

Both of them.

"Is something missing?" Theo asked.

Dino shrugged on his jacket. "I probably just misplaced the papers for my offshore accounts and the transfers from them last month. I'll find them."

"The records of transfers *into* your businesses?"

"Glad you're seeing the problem," Dino muttered.

Theo's brow furrowed. "I can look around and see if it is misplaced."

"Sure, just keep people out of this office when I'm not around."

"I didn't let anyone in, Dino."

Theo *was* the main person running the strip club, though, and that was by Dino's recent decisions to keep him busy. So should someone have gotten in and found the *few* papers that would give inside details and numbers as to his illegal cash flow and how he was pillowing it into legal businesses to hide the funds, then it wouldn't be on Theo's head. Dino was the one allowing his brother control over who came in and out.

Dino would have to answer for shit that went wrong.

"It's fine," Dino said. "I'm sure it'll show up."

"All right."

"And lay off the complaining, Theo. I'm only making you work for your own benefit."

Theo scowled, but wisely chose not to argue. "Yeah, I know."

"I'm heading out, shoot me a message if you need something," Dino told his brother as he passed him in the doorway.

"Sure."

Dino kept his head down as he exited the strip club. The business was just starting to open, so while the girls were beginning to take the stage, and patrons were being frisked at the door before being allowed entrance. He took the corner of the building, still watching his step instead of what was in front of him, and headed toward where he had parked his car earlier in the alley, beside the building.

Pulling the key fob from his pocket, he hit the unlock, and his car's horn beeped twice.

It was only then that he saw who was sitting on the back of his white Bentley.

Karen.

Dino's steps stumbled as he came to a quick stop, surprised to see her there.

He hadn't contacted her in two weeks—since the meeting where he'd flaked on her offer after already agreeing. He figured she wouldn't *want* to hear from him, given how rude it was of him to behave like he had, and he was still trying to keep Ben out of his private business.

That was hard to do when she just showed up like she did.

"What are you doing here?" he asked.

A greeting might have been nice.

An apology probably would have been better.

Dino flinched inwardly at how harsh his question had come out.

"The least you could do if you're done with a person—*me*—is give me a heads up, Dino," Karen said.

She pushed off the back of his car, her heeled boots clicking on the pavement. The skirt of her dress flew up just an inch or two, exposing her legs before it fell back in place. She tightened her coat around her frame, never once taking that icy glare off his form ten feet away.

Dino didn't blame her, or fault her for the anger.

He deserved it.

"I never said I was done," Dino replied. "I've just been—"

"What, busy?" Karen scoffed. "So busy that you couldn't even be bothered to send me a message and let me know? Or how about the fact you've ignored my calls when I actually needed your opinion on things for the restaurant? I could see the personal side of things, Dino. I am more than capable of doing my *job* and turning cheek to the fact you can't even let me know you're done with the other stuff. But you can't even do that."

The strangest sensation crawled over Dino's shoulders. He knew it wasn't because of Karen's words, but rather, his anxiety that rarely left.

It felt like someone was watching him.

And her.

"You shouldn't be here," Dino said.

Karen just stared at him, wary and exhausted. "That's all you have to say? What, are you worried someone might see me and think the stripper is back?"

Ouch.

"No, that's not it at all."

"Right—whatever." Karen walked forward, strolling straight on past Dino without so much as a look at him. Over her shoulder, she called, "Have a great night, Dino. You don't need to say anything, I hear you loud and clear."

The words to keep her there, to explain why he'd been ignoring her calls and staying away, were right on the tip of his tongue. Dino damn near turned on his heel and shouted them just because he *didn't* want her to walk away, but the sad fact was, he knew it was better for her that she did leave him behind.

It was only after he heard tires squeal on wet pavement, signaling Karen had left in her own vehicle, did he actually move toward his car again. He'd just pulled the driver's door open when a familiar form slipped around the side of the building.

Theo leaned against the brick wall, a cigarette hanging from his mouth. "Hey."

Dino wondered just how much his brother had heard. "Don't you have a job to be doing instead of spying on me, Theo?"

"Who was that?"

"Mind your business."

Theo wasn't letting it go that easy. "Isn't that the same woman that was here a couple of months ago looking for a job?"

Jesus.

Dino sent up a silent prayer to God, asking for the man upstairs to cut him some fucking slack. Didn't he have enough shit going on right now without adding his brother's snooping to the mix? It wasn't that Theo meant any harm—Dino was well aware of that. The bigger problem was that without even meaning to, Theo might cause both Dino and Karen problems simply by *knowing* there was something going on under the radar of certain people.

People like *Ben*.

"Mind your business," Dino said again, firmer the second time.

Theo took a drag off his cigarette, letting the heavy smoke billow into the air before he asked, "So, is that where your time has been going lately? I didn't know you were involved with someone."

"I'm not."

"I've never seen her before either," Theo went on, ignoring his brother's refusals, "except for that one time here, of course."

"Theo—"

"She's an ... outsider?"

Dino cringed, glancing away to hide the truth. That was the one question he didn't want asked or wondered about where Karen was concerned. "Theo, leave it alone. She's nobody—she sure as hell doesn't need to *be* somebody. Nothing is going on that you need to concern yourself with. Keep your mouth shut that you saw *anything*. Understand?"

Theo nodded, though he didn't look pleased about it. "Shouldn't keep secrets like those, Dino. Secrets don't stay hidden for long—we both know that. Bad shit happens when people in this family keep secrets, remember?"

"For fuck's sake, Theo—"

His brother threw his hands up, tossing his cigarette to the ground at the same time. "Nobody, I got it. See you whenever, brother."

Dino's gaze narrowed on his brother's back as he watched Theo head back around the corner of the club. He wasn't all too worried about Theo starting some kind of shit over what he saw, or what he thought he might know about Dino's involvement with a woman outside of Outfit business and the families. Theo wasn't the type, as far as that went.

But he had to be careful.

Especially so.

Dino climbed into his Bentley, desperately trying to ignore the headache beginning to form in his temples. If someone in the Outfit, or his asshole of an uncle, didn't kill him first, the stress he was under would surely do the goddamn job.

Quickly, Dino got on the road, and onto the highway, pressing the gas pedal down harder, using the speed of his car and the focus it took to weave in and out of vehicles to keep his crazy thoughts and his suffocating anxiety at bay.

It seemed like his life was blackening all over again.

The edges were slowly moving in on him.

He hated that.

The one happy place he had found, the few quiet moments that never took more than he could give, was being withheld from him now.

Karen.

Dino wasn't sure how to deal with it all, really.

It was only after Dino passed a familiar Chinese restaurant did he realize that his heart was speaking louder than his brain.

He hadn't even driven himself home.

He wasn't even going in the right direction.

Apparently, he was going to be apologizing to someone tonight. Although, he wasn't quite sure how Karen would feel when he showed up on her apartment's doorstep after their earlier showdown.

Not even telling himself that seemed to help.

He was still driving in her direction.

Dino pulled into a corner store, knowing he was going to need to come with his hands full. An offer of a truce, maybe.

She did like her wine and chocolate.

And you, he told himself. *She likes you.*

There was that, too.

CHAPTER 10

KNOCKING on the door, Dino took a wide step back to let Karen see him through the peephole. He held his offerings up for her to see—Chinese food, chocolate, and wine. He knew she was home, if only because her car was in the apartment's underground garage. Besides that, during the time they had spent together, he noticed things about Karen.

She was a homebody.

She didn't have a lot of friends.

She liked her privacy.

Dino related to all of those things, and maybe that was why, even knowing Karen was going to be pissed off at him when she opened her apartment door, he was still drawn here.

Drawn to her.

His smile grew as he heard footsteps approach the closed door, and then it faded when nothing happened. He didn't hear the telltale clang of the lock chain being unlocked, or even the slide of the deadbolt.

But he also didn't hear her footsteps retreat again.

That was a good thing.

Dino took that as she wasn't sending him away and rejecting him.

Yet.

Glancing at the peephole, he had the distinct feeling Karen was watching him, and probably going back and forth about what she should do.

He didn't blame her a bit.

"I'm sort of shitty at this whole thing," Dino said quietly, aware that she could hear him even at a lower tone. Her apartment building didn't offer very much privacy where noise was concerned. He cringed when he added, "You know, being a decent human being and all. And you were right earlier. I absolutely could have called you or let you know I needed to drop off your radar for a while, and I should have. There's no excuse for why I didn't."

He shifted on his feet, not quite finished.

"But you were wrong about something else, Karen," he continued, never once looking away from the peephole as he spoke, "I'm not *finished* with you or whatever it is we're doing together. That had nothing to do with why I went silent for a while. I'm not done here—with you, I mean. So if you're not done, then open the door, and let's have that night I missed a couple of weeks ago."

The chain clanged as it was pulled and the deadbolt unlatched loudly.

Dino took a slight step back as Karen slowly pulled the door of the apartment open, as the last thing he wanted to seem was imposing.

Leaning against the doorjamb, Karen stood in one of her oversized T-shirts that doubled as a nightie when she slept. She put a hand to her hip, and for a long while, only stared at Dino waiting in the hallway, never saying a thing or even moving to invite him in.

Finally, she did speak.

It felt like a giant battle won to Dino.

"You know, I think that's the most you've ever said to me at one time," Karen admitted.

There was a hint of sadness in her words.

Dino wasn't quite sure how to make it go away. "I'm not a big talker."

"Are you going to give me an actual reason *why* you went AWOL on me?"

Yeah, there it was.

"Things got busy and—"

Karen held up a single hand, stopping him from saying more. "You're lying. That's an excuse, not a real reason. I'm not interested in having a deflection, Dino."

He didn't know how to give her the truth.

He didn't want to expose her to the monster she invited into her bed or the life he kept hidden across town.

It was the most selfish thing he could do, and Dino knew that all too well. He should give her the chance to decide if his lifestyle and the choices that came with it was something she wanted to be involved in, even if her only involvement was just limited to her time spent in private with him.

But he couldn't do it.

Because what if she shut him out?

What if she pushed him away?

What if he lost the sunlight she brought to him?

That wasn't a risk Dino was willing to take.

He also didn't want to lie, so he gave her the next best thing.

"Sometimes I'm going to need to do that," Dino explained. "Go, and not give a reason. Stay away, and then show back up when it's good again. I can't give you more than what I offer, Karen, and what I'm offering is what you've already seen. So if you're not happy with it, or you want more than what I've given already, let me know. I only need to know where you stand so I can do what I need to do."

All over again, she watched him.

Silent and pensive.

Sad and still.

She wasn't like him, and maybe that was the hardest part. Karen's days were full of her bright, easy-going personality, and the light that always seemed to follow her around. Dino was the exact opposite—blackened at his edges, a coldness constantly seeping from his exterior that matched the tar in his soul.

He was a shadow.

Walked over.

Passed by.

Looked beyond.

He couldn't begin to understand how they were ever supposed to work, given how entirely different their worlds were from the outside looking in.

Dino still wanted to try.

Karen took a deep breath, her arms crossing over her chest as she looked him over again. "You're aware that half of the hallway are probably standing with their ears pressed to the door, listening to you right now."

Dino managed a smile for her. "They're not the ones keeping me out here."

"True. This is probably the most entertainment they've had in a while."

"You only have to tell me to leave, Karen."

"I'm aware, Dino."

She reached out and grabbed the wine and chocolate from his hands instead. Then, she stepped to the side, and let him in.

As Dino walked into the comfort of her apartment, where he could see marks of her life every which way he turned, he wondered how long it would be before he was forced out of it again.

Karen leaned over Dino's shoulder, her lips pressing sweetly to his cheek as she placed a coffee to the small table in front of him. Steam lifted in dancing ribbons from the black coffee, smelling wonderful and demanding his attention.

He'd drink it in a minute.

Something else was taking up his interest.

Turning just enough to catch Karen's mouth with his own, he felt her smile grow against the kiss.

"Morning," she said, the gravely hoarseness of sleep coloring up her greeting.

Dino kissed her forehead. "Morning, sweetheart."

He turned his attention back to his task and Karen stretched up on her tiptoes before heading back to the kitchen. She was back at his side in less than a few seconds, placing her own coffee down beside his. The milky cream color swirling around in hers was a stark contrast against the blackened bitterness of his.

Karen practically fell into the couch beside him, tucking in close to his side and pulling her legs up tight. Dino passed her coffee over without even needing to be asked, knowing she would want it first and foremost.

She had several routines that got her through the day.

He figured her morning one was most important, though.

Dino continued sketching out lines and shadowing in curves on the notepad with a sharpened pencil as Karen sipped happily and silently from her coffee, never once interrupting his work. She wouldn't, he knew, not until she'd downed at least half of the caffeine she needed to actually feel awake.

He knew she was close to reaching the halfway point in her coffee when she shifted beside him, finding a more comfortable spot and stretching her beautiful legs out to rest her feet on the arm while crossing her ankles. Her arm hung over his knee, her fingertips grazing softly back and forth over his bare calf, rhythmic and gentle.

They'd done this before; quiet mornings and soft touches.

It was one of his favorite things to do with Karen.

Oddly, it allowed him to just be in that moment with no expectations but sunlight filtering in through the window and the silence stretching on between them until she was ready to talk.

The image he was drawing—a memory that had haunted him the night before as he walked the floors of Karen's apartment— was beginning to take shape. He didn't think he was particularly good at drawing, but it was calming. Sometimes it even helped to remove the awful demons living inside his head, if only long enough for him to put them to paper.

It never failed to amaze Dino how easily and peacefully Karen slept night after night. Since showing up at her place, he'd fought with himself about leaving again, and his heart ended up winning the battle. He stayed one night, then two. She went off to work that Monday morning, not even bothering to ask him if he would be there when she got back.

Dino figured she already knew and didn't need to ask.

Of course he was there.

He only left to grab some of the pastries she liked from the shop down the street.

Karen never once noticed his odd habits at night, and if she did, she never said a word about them. Watching her sleep, tangled in blankets with messed hair and a lax smile, was probably the closest he'd ever come to actually *wanting* to crawl into a bed and close his eyes.

If only because she looked so peaceful there.

It would, however, be selfish of him to get in bed with her, only to wake her up with his nightmares, something he wasn't quite ready to explain just yet.

His body was starting to feel the exhaustion of three nights with no solid sleep. He'd caught a couple of hours during the day, but it wasn't enough to keep him distracted from the tiredness seeping into his system every time he turned around.

If he were at home, he could distract himself with all sorts of things. Being at Karen's place meant he couldn't fiddle around, or change and reorganize her cupboards and drawers, and he was pretty sure she wouldn't appreciate him cleaning her place from top to bottom, even if the action would have literally nothing to do with the cleanliness of her place.

The apartment didn't need it anyway.

Karen kept the place spotless.

Dino still needed a distraction.

Well, the truth of the matter was simple. Despite how much he wanted to stay, if even for one more night, he was going to have to leave. He'd have to battle through a good night's worth of nightmares because he was too tired to ignore the rest he desperately needed.

He was not looking forward to that.

Dino pushed all of those thoughts out of his mind, focusing instead on the graze of Karen's fingertips to his skin and her soft breaths as he continued sketching on the pad. The actions, her touch, the sounds, and his focus, all bled together, lulling him into a sense of comfort he hadn't expected.

He was sure Karen was done her coffee, and surely she was ready to start her day like she usually did once the cup in her hands was empty, but she never moved from the couch. Actually, she shifted her position again, allowing her head to rest into his side as she faced away from him, her empty coffee mug sitting snugly in her grasp.

He didn't even realize his gaze was dropping and the swipes of his pencil was slowing. His own breathing had also calmed, nearly matching the slow inhales and exhales of his companion curled up like a happy little kitten at his side. She was so warm, her heat bleeding into his body and taking him even further into the still abyss settling into his brain.

It was hard to know one was asleep, Dino recognized all too

late, when all that found him in that usually dark place … was peace.

CHAPTER
11

DINO'S eyes flew open and he jerked into a straight sitting position at the sound of a door clicking shut. As quiet as the sound was, it still jarred through every nerve ending in his body as if it was a spike being driven into his skull.

At first he stood up, his hands reaching for the gun he usually kept hidden in a holster at his back, but he came up empty. At the same time, he realized he wasn't wearing his jacket, his dress shirt was unbuttoned all the way down his chest, and he was only in his boxer-briefs.

It took far too many minutes of him standing there, blinking and looking like a fucking fool before he realized where he was and what must have happened.

Karen's cozy, one-bedroom apartment stared back at him. The black screen of the television was just feet away, still turned off like he had left it that morning. On the table sat his full cup of untouched—likely cold, now—coffee that she had brought him, as well as his notepad and pencil, both resting side by side as if waiting for him to pick them back up and continue with his drawing.

"You're awake," Karen said, gliding on past his position to head for the kitchen.

Dino looked over his shoulder at her, taking note of the fact she was dressed for the day, with her beige trench coat cinched tight at her waist and her black heeled boots clicking on the linoleum floor. Hanging from each of her hands were bags—plastic bags from the grocery store.

"You seemed tired," she said, hefting the bags onto the kitchen table without so much as a glance in his direction.

She had no idea of the war raging inside his head.

Had she just left him there to sleep?

How had he just ... *slept?*

Dino couldn't remember a single time where he had slept without some kind of nightmare waking him up. The dreams could range from anxiety-inducing, to downright hell. He'd tried everything from medication to getting drunk as shit in an effort to ward off the nightmares before falling asleep, and yet nothing had worked.

Except ... something had.

"You must have been tired," Karen continued on, unloading groceries from the bag and setting the items aside. "It's almost supper time, Dino."

He glanced at the clock on the wall, taking in the time and realizing she wasn't exaggerating in the slightest. He had slept all fucking day. *Hours*—all of them without the triggering pain that could and would leave him mentally debilitated for *days*.

"You all right?"

Dino looked to Karen, hearing her question and trying to figure out the right way to answer it. A notch appeared between her eyebrows, the first sign of her concern. She wasn't a stupid woman, and he wasn't about to treat her like one, so he wasn't surprised that she noticed something was ... off.

"No," Dino said, though even the word came out hesitant. "Nothing is wrong."

It *was* true.

Was he supposed to complain about the fact he was awake, not the least bit tired, and his mind wasn't filled with the lingering aftereffects of his horrible upbringing?

Because he didn't think so.

It was just strange.

"Okay," Karen said, seeming rather chipper as she went about her task.

She unloaded what was left of the groceries quickly, taking a few vegetables to the sink to rinse them off before grabbing some cookware from the cupboards. Dino eventually came to stand in the entryway of the kitchen, leaning against the wall and watching her work. She was smooth about it all, never bothered by his presence or calling him out on his silence.

It was only after she'd began chopping the red and green peppers did she finally turn to him.

"My father has insomnia," she said.

He was well aware that statement didn't come out of the blue.

"I don't," he offered blandly.

Karen frowned, her gaze turning back on her task as she swiped strips of the cut peppers into a small bowl before setting them aside. "You've probably spent what, a couple weeks' worth of nights at my place, right?"

Dino shrugged. "Probably. Why?"

"You do realize you're not a small statured man, yeah?"

"Get to the point, Karen."

She gave him a pensive look over her shoulder that told him to cut the attitude without even saying a word out loud. It wasn't that he meant to be rude, but Dino knew exactly where this conversation was leading to, and he wasn't sure that he wanted to have it with her.

At least, not right now.

He wasn't saying never—just not in that moment.

Apparently, Karen was not even close to being on the same wavelength as Dino.

"You walk the halls a lot at night," Karen said, keeping her back turned to him. "I've caught you a couple of times when you're just staring out the window, and I've even called your name, but you didn't answer me."

Dino's throat tightened at the revelation.

Sometimes, he didn't even need to sleep for the memories to suffocate him.

Sometimes, the darkness of the night was enough to do the deed.

"I don't have insomnia," Dino repeated, firmer the second time.

Karen nodded, but didn't reply.

His words were the truth.

Falling asleep and staying asleep were not the problems for him.

It was what happened when he was already there and couldn't get himself awake again.

"You *did* seem quite peaceful earlier," Karen said softly, still working away, "and I could tell you were tired when I woke up this morning, so I didn't want to wake you."

"That's fair."

"Was it a good sleep?"

Her question was innocent enough.

"It was, actually," he admitted.

Karen turned then, a brilliant smile coloring up her features. The sunlight coming in through the small kitchen window almost created a haloed effect around her small form.

If Dino was ever asked to give just one thing to describe what happiness *looked* like to him, it would be Karen in that moment.

The feeling was profound to him.

Almost foreign.

"Hungry?" she asked.

"I could eat," he replied, "if you're cooking."

Karen laughed, winking before she turned back to the counter. "Lay that charm on, Dino. You know how much I like it."

He'd never quite thought of himself as charming before.

But it *had* made her smile again.

Tucked into the corner of the couch, his notepad and pencil back in his hands as he put more detail, more of his memories of the moment he was currently drawing onto the paper, Dino found himself watching Karen again.

She was engrossed in the series marathon playing on television. Her brief bouts of laughter occasionally brought his attention back to her before the moment was gone and he was back to his drawing.

Dino was all too aware that he couldn't ignore the outside world forever. He couldn't keep himself locked up in Karen's apartment for much longer, because someone might finally notice he hadn't been around.

It wasn't as if he'd missed anything important. There were no meetings he needed to attend, and his business dealings were being handled by other people, while he'd left the immediate work to his younger brother.

He didn't really need to go.

Dino worried that pushing his luck might not end well for him.

Tomorrow, he'd head back to his place, and make sure he was seen by the people who needed to see him. That left him with one more night, and oddly, he hoped it was a dreamless one.

"Dino?"

"Yeah, sweetheart?"

He glanced up at Karen's call of his name, realizing he'd zoned out again while going back and forth between drawing and watching her. She was such an interesting creature. To some, she probably seemed overtly *normal*. Nothing extraordinarily special about a woman who could be set beside a hundred other women and not stand out in the crowd.

Dino didn't think that was true at all.

Anyone who might think that of Karen was missing out on the beauty that radiated from her easy smile and warm eyes.

She couldn't possibly be just normal.

Not when she was as wonderful as she was.

Karen leaned over a bit, coming closer to his spot at the other end of the couch. "Are you almost done?"

"Done what?"

"Drawing, Dino. That's what you've been doing for the last two hours."

He looked to the clock—had it been that long?

Smirking, Dino set his pad and pencil aside. "Maybe it's the company that keeps me occupied and losing time."

Karen's cheeks pinked slightly. "Was that a come-on?"

"Not—"

"Because you know all you really need to do is tell me you want to fuck, right?"

Dino's brow lifted at her blatant suggestion. "Good to know, but that's not what I was trying to do."

"Boo, you're no fun. Can I see your drawing then?"

At that request, Dino did hesitate.

Karen was quick to notice. "You don't have to. I was just curious."

He wasn't sure that she would understand the sketch he'd been working on all day, or for that matter, if she would recognize the battered face staring back at her in the image. The brutality that he'd drawn onto the white page was disconcerting in detail, even to his eye and mind, the very person who had lived it.

"It's ..." Dino stopped whatever he was going to say, knowing it was better if he didn't refuse her, if only to *share* something. He didn't share a lot with Karen, not that she asked him to. It was one of her many wonderful qualities. "Here."

He passed the notepad over, turning his attention to the television as he dropped his pencil to the coffee table. For a long while, he waited for Karen to say something—*anything* at all about the image on the paper.

He didn't need to look at the drawing to know what it was, and he wasn't quite sure how realistically detailed he had managed to get the image. Honestly, he didn't really need to, not when his own mind could conjure up the very same moment in time as though he were being shoved back into it.

Blood in his mouth.

Busted lips.

Blackened eyes.

Bruises forming.

Wet pavement.

Dead eyes.

... and a booted foot coming down, readying to connect another violent kick.

He could remember every single vile second of that beating on the night his parents were killed inside their home. And while he couldn't put the sounds to paper, he could hear his uncle in the background, encouraging the men to continue with their assault. Or his much younger siblings, crying as they were dragged further away from the love and safety he wanted to give to them in a moment that was nothing more than a nightmare.

He hadn't put the other details into the drawing—ones like the flashing lights of the police cruisers, or the officers standing nearby, their backs turned to hide from the violence happening just behind them.

Finally, Dino heard the soft thump of the notepad being tossed to the coffee table. It was only a second later before Karen was crawling into his lap without a word, her soft hands finding his skin and somehow—*some-fucking-how*—calming the racing flood of pain and anxiety that coursed through his veins.

"Not insomnia," she murmured against his neck.

Dino cleared his throat of the thickness building there. "No, it's definitely not that."

Her lips pressed to his pulse point, and he wrapped his arms around her waist, wanting to keep her there a bit longer.

Still, she shifted in his embrace, turning to sit with her back flush against his chest. Reaching over, Karen grabbed the notepad and the drawing, resting it on her lap as she stared down at it again.

"It *is* hauntingly beautiful," she said, her voice barely breaking a whisper. "It's awful, you know, but it's amazing at the same time."

"I see it more like a nightmare."

She couldn't possibly know how true his statement was.

"Why do I have a feeling this is just one of *many*?" Karen asked.

Dino let his fingers tangle into the waves of her hair, pulling her closer to press a kiss to her temple. "You *did* think I was a little strange."

"I never asked why, though."

"You didn't really have to."

CHAPTER 12

THE home of the Outfit boss—Terrance Trentini—was a sprawling estate with two wings, set upon land that was perfectly manicured and always *watched*. It didn't seem to matter to Dino if it was his first or fiftieth time visiting the mansion, he managed to feel like a bug under a microscope just standing in the driveway.

The mansion, as looming as it seemed, was lit up on the inside and outside with dancing twinkle lights meant to help celebrate the occasion.

Someone's birthday, Dino knew.

One of Terrance's granddaughters, likely.

He didn't pay that much attention to the occasion when Ben had called with the invitation, though it had been more like a demand. He had brought a generic birthday card with money shoved inside and his signature scrawled across the bottom. It would have to do.

The inside of the mansion, decorated in gold, black, and pink, confirmed Dino's belief that the celebration had something to do with the Trentini girls. He did the appropriate thing, which meant greeting anyone he saw, as he made his way to the gift table and added his to the hugely growing pile.

The place was filled with Outfit people.

It was also the very last place Dino wanted to be.

He found a quiet corner away from the bulk of the chatting guests, and tried to stay out of the way for the most part. It was easier to do with a drink in his hand, so when a server walked past with a tray of poured whiskeys, Dino was quick to grab one and down over half of it in a single gulp.

The burn of the liquor sliding down his throat was heavenly.

He eyed the people as they mingled, wishing he was far across town in a quiet apartment that didn't belong to him with a brown-eyed girl that somehow managed to make him feel far more content in his own skin than these people ever had.

Dino had grown up being told the Outfit was his family, and so, he should treat it as such and protect it the same way. He'd never understood that sentiment.

How could he, when it seemed like the only thing the Outfit had ever done for Dino—or even his siblings, really—had been to hurt them?

Murdering his parents …

Leaving them orphans …

Pretending they didn't know the monsters they were left with …

Uncaring if they did know …

It was a strange mindset to have—to care for these people as if they were his *family*.

"You're awfully quiet over here," Ben said as he leaned back into the wall, mimicking Dino's position. "I barely noticed you."

Dino had known his uncle was approaching, if only because it was damn near impossible to *not* see Ben DeLuca in a crowd, but he had ignored the man, hoping he would overlook him. Clearly, he had hoped for too much.

"Having a drink," Dino said, lifting his glass to show the few sips of whiskey he had left.

"Shame your sister is missing this," Ben mused.

Dino resisted the urge to roll his eyes, instead taking a drink to get the burn in his throat again to keep him quiet.

"Lily would enjoy this," Ben continued.

Dino couldn't stay quiet at that. "Lily would hate something like this."

Ben's brow lifted. "Being celebrated and treated like a princess?"

"Being in the spotlight."

A dry chuckle escaped Ben.

"Well, she would learn to like it, I suppose."

Dino hid his frown by looking away, knowing that wasn't true but unwilling to argue the point any further with Ben. No matter what he said, Ben was stuck in his beliefs, and it was pointless to attempt any change.

"Speaking of Lily," Ben continued, clearly unaware of Dino's lack of attention to the conversation, "have you spoken to her?"

"Briefly," Dino said.

That was a lie.

Over the last few months, Lily's calls had dissipated into practically nothing at all. The postcards she sent each time she arrived somewhere new, had also slowed down—going from three a month, to one every couple of months if Dino was lucky. He wasn't worried about his sister, as far as that went, but it did bother him on some level.

Lily had left Chicago because she *wanted* to get away. She wanted to leave the Outfit and the people behind, and she didn't want to be stuck here, living for what benefited the family, instead of what benefited her.

She'd long held a grudge where the Outfit was concerned for taking away her mother and father, and the dreams and ideals she'd held as a child.

Dino understood that had to be painful for his sister.

He figured—though not from being told from Lily herself— that after finally being given some freedom, that grudge she held was finally allowed to grow. He imagined it was easier to hate people when they weren't staring you right in the face.

Lily would never admit it herself, but Dino was all too aware of what she was doing.

Running.

Running from her past and the Outfit.

Keeping herself happy by staying away.

Forcing herself into the constant present so she never had to deal with the past.

He figured no harm, no foul.

Lily had no need to come back to Chicago, at least not from Dino's perspective, and so he would let her run.

For now.

"And?" Ben pressed, bringing Dino back to the conversation at hand.

"And what, Ben?"

"Where was she the last time you spoke?"

Dino lied, because he couldn't remember. "A small town

outside of Italy. She was lodging there before she went off again."

"Funny."

A trickle of unease crawled down Dino's spine. "What?"

"Carmela was talking to Lily a few days ago—she called the house trying to find a number for Theo," Ben stated rather absently.

Dino knew Ben's flippant demeanor was a lie.

"She could have called me," Dino replied.

It was the best he could come up with at the moment.

Ben didn't seem like he cared. "She's been in Germany for a while."

Shit.

"I said 'the last time.'"

"How long has it been since the last time, Dino?" Ben asked, not even giving Dino a chance to respond before he continued on speaking. "Apparently long enough that you don't even realize your sister has changed *countries*. I've had quite enough of this—her traveling unchaperoned and freely, for that matter. Bring her home."

"Ben—"

His uncle pushed away from the wall, giving Dino a cold look over his shoulder that said this was not up for discussion between them. "You'll bring her home, or I'll force her back."

The threat hung heavily between the two men.

Dino's grip on his glass tightened enough that he feared it might shatter in his palm.

Still, he stood his ground. "I'm not bringing her home yet."

Ben's gaze narrowed. "Repeat that again, Dino."

"She doesn't need to be here. She's fine where she is. I'm not bringing her home."

"Are you sure that is the road you want to travel with me?"

Not at all.

Dino was more than certain this wasn't going to end well for him.

Anytime in the past that he had refused Ben's wishes had almost always ended rather violently for Dino. Broken bones. A battered, bloody body. His mind in tatters, much like his mental health.

There was a reason Dino was so shut off from the world and often debilitated by the nightmares living inside his head.

Ben was every single one of those reasons.

His uncle's way of making sure Dino learned his lesson the first time, as to ensure the next time he would get what he wanted, was to beat the lesson into him. Quite literally.

It didn't even matter to Dino.

Not now.

He was more than willing to take a lesson from Ben as long as the end result was the same. Lily stayed where she was because Dino allowed it, whether Ben liked it or not. His sister *was not* going to be fodder for Ben's games. She had always been free and safe from their uncle and aunt's abuse—she would remain free and safe from it as long as Dino had his say.

This was his say.

"Let me tell you something," Ben said as he turned to face Dino, leaving his back to the crowd.

Dino pushed away from the wall, stopping only a half of a foot from his uncle's frame. Despite Ben's age, he was still a rather intimidating man in height and stature. His dark eyes could quickly shut someone up without ever having to speak a word. It was almost as though the man could promise violence with a look, and Dino knew what was promised, was always *gifted*.

He still didn't care.

Not on this.

This, he wouldn't move even an inch.

"No, let me tell you something," Dino replied, never once looking away from his uncle. "I know a few things where Lily is concerned, things that you are not aware of. Like the fact she won't be easy to find because she doesn't stay in one town for long. Or the fact that the only time you might get a hit off of her is when her passport gets dinged from traveling into a new country because the accounts I set up for her to use have *fuck all* to do with the accounts you have access to. That is, when she happens to use accounts at all, because she likes cash far more, and we both know how damned hard it is to track cash, Ben."

Ben's glare burned, but Dino didn't back down.

He couldn't.

"I let her go because she wanted to, because she deserved to have *her* time," Dino said firmly, never allowing even the hint of his nerves to show in his tone. If he did, Ben was liable to pick up on it and use it to hurt Dino with in some way. They'd done this before—many times. Very rarely did it end to Dino's favor, but he had to at least *try*. For Lily. "And when she is done with having that time for herself, or when I am ready to call her back, then I will do just that. But not *one* fucking second before, Ben."

"That feels like a challenge," Ben murmured.

Dino's jaw ached from clenching so hard. "I'm not budging on this."

"Seems there's a lot you won't budge on lately, Dino."

He didn't grace that with a response.

It didn't seem to matter all that much to Ben.

"No matter," Ben said, tossing one hand high as if to wave the whole conversation away. "Seems interesting to me how you've forgotten what denying me will earn you, Dino. Haven't I gotten that stubborn trait of yours disposed of already?"

Dino's throat thickened at the veiled threat. "Beaten out of me."

Ben smiled. "Call it what you want, Dino."

"I call it what it *is*."

"So be it. Fact is, you still haven't learned."

Dino pushed past Ben, the threat hanging over his shoulder as he moved in and out of people. He could feel Ben's words biting at his back, looking for a chunk to rip out.

Words were nothing.

Words meant *nothing*.

Except when it was Ben saying them.

Dino was all too aware, given the number of scars he sported under his clothes and the aches in his bones on rainy days, of just how powerful Ben's words could be.

Ignoring the faces and waving hands trying to draw Dino into conversations, he kept walking, making his way to the front of the mansion where he picked his jacket out of the coat room and pulled his car keys from the pocket. He was just walking out the front door when his shoulder rammed into a solid form.

Dino was stuck too far inside his own head to care.

He needed to get out of there.

He needed to prepare for the hell that was about to come his way.

It was inevitable …

It always came.

"Shit, Dino," Theo grumbled. "Watch where you're going."

It was only the sound of his brother's annoyance that stopped Dino from going to his car and getting the hell out of there. Ben would never do something in such a public way that attention would be drawn to him. No, he'd wait for when night fell, when Dino was alone, and then he would strike.

Or send someone to do his dirty business for him.

Still, when it came to Theo, he had to stop.

Like his sister, Dino protected his brother.

He tried, anyway. As much as he could. Theo often didn't know that's what Dino was doing, but that was fine, too.

Turning to face his brother, Dino schooled his features. He didn't want Theo picking up on the fact something was wrong, or that anything had happened. He wanted to keep Theo out of his business with Ben as much as possible.

God knew Theo had taken his shit, too.

He'd been through hell, too.

"If Ben asks about Lily, you don't know a goddamn thing," Dino said.

Theo's brow furrowed, and he let the mansion door close, blocking their conversation from being overheard by anyone inside. "I don't know anything about Lily. I haven't talked to her in—shit, months, maybe?"

"She's going to call. Don't answer. Don't get information that Ben can use. If you don't know something, you can't tell him something."

"Why—"

"Do as I said."

Theo's features hardened, his annoyance back in a blink. "She doesn't call me anyway. There's nothing for me to know to tell him. What is your fucking problem?"

"This whole fucking family."

"*What?*"

Dino couldn't be bothered to explain it.

His whole damn life was the problem.

Theo should understand, but he wasn't like Dino. He'd never been like his brother.

Dino took care of them all, watching out for his siblings even when it was to the detriment of his own self. He'd never once expected them to look out for him.

That was his job.

"Just … do what I said," Dino told his brother one last time. "And next week, lay low. You could use the break, right? I've put a lot on you. Take a break."

That would keep Theo out of harm's way.

Surely.

He heard Theo's confirmation behind him, but he was already walking away.

CHAPTER 13

FOR the next week, Dino bounced from business to business, never staying in one place for very long. During the daytime hours, he'd make use of one of the back offices in his three restaurants, and later in the evening, he'd travel to the strip club to close out his day.

As time passed, without Ben's warning coming to any kind of fruition, Dino started to get paranoid. It was unlike his uncle to sit so long on his anger without some kind of action.

It didn't bode well for Dino.

That, or Ben was simply waiting for when Dino was not looking over his shoulder.

The fact that Dino was an adult—a grown man capable of making his own decisions—did not factor to Ben at all. His uncle's only goal where his family was concerned was the same goal it had always been: to control.

Ben controlled his family by whatever means necessary.

Usually, by violence and fear.

Dino had grown accustomed to the lessons his uncle provided over the years. He was never surprised to walk out of his office or apartment to find a man with a baseball bat waiting before waking up confused and bloody.

It was why he didn't understand the lack of action now.

Ben wouldn't stand for disobedience of any sort—certainly not a refusal of his wants.

Dino had done that, and blatantly so.

To his uncle, he'd probably *earned* whatever was coming.

He just didn't understand why it hadn't come yet.

"You okay?"

Dino's head popped up at Karen's soft voice. Leaning against the brick wall of the restaurant's alleyway, he'd found a quiet place to think. He took a final drag from his cigarette, and then tossed it to the wet pavement, giving Karen a fleeting smile.

"Fine. Aren't you supposed to be working?"

Karen cocked a brow at him. "I *do* get breaks, don't I?"

Dino chuckled. "You know you do."

"Well, I'm using this one to check on you. You've been quiet today."

"I'm always quiet, Karen."

"True, but you talk to me."

She had him there.

Dino didn't want her worrying over him, though, so he deflected her questions in the best way he could. "Something was off in the Accounts Receivable for last month. The numbers didn't add up. I need you to go back over the ledgers again before the numbers get logged in."

Karen sighed. "You know my numbers are good, Dino."

They were.

She was damn good at keeping the books.

Or cooking them to hide shit, for that matter.

Still, he was the boss.

Her lover, sure, but the boss just the same.

"Look over them again," he said with a shrug. "Maybe it was just my eyes that saw something that wasn't there."

Karen gave him another one of her looks, then finally nodded. "All right."

Dino checked his watch, noting the time. He had been trying to stay away from this particular restaurant as much as possible this week, just in case, but that hadn't worked out very well for him that morning when he'd woken up with an ache in his chest. An ache he couldn't really explain, but left him feeling cold and lonely in a way he hadn't experienced before.

He knew instantly what it was.

He missed Karen.

It was almost *too* easy for him to get in his car and decide he'd work out of the restaurant where she worked for the day. It was almost strange the way the ache calmed the very second he was driving in her direction, knowing he was just minutes from seeing her.

Dino had a pretty good grasp on how messed up he was, but when he put Karen into the picture, it was almost as if all of that craziness went away for a time. He didn't have to be the Outfit man, the no nonsense Capo, or the brother trying to keep his siblings safe and clear of pain and manipulation.

He just had to be him.

That was all Karen knew.

It was all she asked for.

Dino liked that a lot.

Problem was, he didn't know how to deal with the way it left him feeling.

Like maybe he was going to have to end whatever he had going on with her because getting too close could be dangerous—but he wasn't sure if it was too dangerous for her, or him.

He was just a mess.

"Do you want to do dinner later?" Karen asked, still hanging out the back exit door.

Dino didn't think on that offer for long, because despite how much he wanted to agree to it, he knew that he couldn't. Not with Ben in a fit and liable to send someone after Dino. Thankfully, no one had ever gotten in the way of one of Ben's lessons, as far as Dino knew, and he didn't want to start now.

Especially not with Karen.

"Raincheck," Dino said, glancing away from Karen's crestfallen face.

He didn't want to see her sadness.

He didn't want her to see his lies.

"Soon, though," he added.

"You sure?"

Dino forced back the stinging sensation prickling at his throat, the words trying to take back what he had said and grab onto what she was offering. It wasn't a good time.

"Soon," Dino repeated.

He frowned at the sight of Karen's back as she disappeared inside the restaurant.

She hadn't even said goodbye.

Dino couldn't blame her, really. How fun could it be to find yourself stuck in a relationship with someone like him who took a great deal from you, but rarely offered the same in return? It wasn't that he meant to be like he was—distant and seemingly selfish— but he didn't know how to *be* anything else.

And hadn't he told her once that all she needed to do was tell him to leave and he would go?

Karen still hadn't told him that yet.

Somewhere deep inside, covered by years of old scar tissue and buried beneath the memories of those wounds, Dino knew the truth was beating hard in his heart.

He seriously hoped she *never* told him that.

Even if it ended up killing him.

Dino considered going back inside the restaurant and apologizing to Karen before leaving for the strip club to finish business for the day, but he decided against it.

Why?

Because he was a fucking coward.

No other explanation was needed.

Strolling down the alleyway toward the mouth of the parking lot, Dino fished in his pocket for the car keys that should be in there. He pulled the keyring out, the jangling keys clamped tightly in his fist as he walked out of the alley.

And looked up to find the butt of a handgun coming straight for his face.

Dino didn't even have time to react before the hard butt of the gun cracked him straight in the mouth, sending him sprawling to the ground with a shout. The taste of blood—tangy and metallic—bloomed in his mouth, making him gag.

It always did.

It reminded him of too many things.

The taste was like a hundred memories swarming his brain all at once.

Overwhelming him …

Choking him …

The second he froze was his biggest mistake. It gave his attacker the extra time he needed to hit again, a foot coming down hard on Dino's rib as the gun slammed into his bloody face once more.

It was unlike Ben to send only *one* person.

Usually it was group of his uncle's enforcers coming to do the dirty work.

It was only when Dino started fighting back did he realize there *was* more men, they had simply been waiting for him to actually do something before deciding whether or not they needed to jump in.

He was dragged back into the alley, hidden from view of the parking lot and the day light. Arms and hands barricaded his limbs, pinning him to the cold, wet ground as feet and fists pounded into him again and again.

Pain flared to life in old spots.

... and new ones.

A gloved hand covered his mouth as a fist drove into his eye, blurring his vision and muddying up his mind with the force of the hit.

The whack of something solid against his side made Dino lose his breath.

Jesus.

Ben was not playing around this time.

Dino waited for the inevitable to come. That blissfully beautiful moment when the blackness finally took over and he didn't *feel* anything. He almost always woke up from the blackness in the same spot he'd been attacked, but sometimes he woke up in a basement if the beating had been particularly bad. If Ben wasn't sure his victim would survive, then he liked to leave them to die in a place where the cleanup would be easy.

Still, Dino struggled with the men his uncle had sent, trying uselessly to protect his face and head through the attack, though it did very little when he was still being held in place.

Through his blurry vision, he couldn't quite make out the faces of the men.

It wouldn't matter, he knew.

Sometimes Ben used his men connected to the Outfit.

Sometimes he used men outside of his connection.

They were paid to do a job.

Nothing more.

Dino was that job.

The worst part was that Dino was more than capable of protecting himself in a fight or attack. He boxed as a teen, and got into more than enough street fights to know how to take care of his shit. He wasn't a small man by any means, and he worked out more than enough to have strength, power, and a quickness about his own attack that most people couldn't see coming until it was too late.

It all meant very little when something like this happened.

Ben knew Dino was *capable*.

He liked proving that when Dino couldn't be capable, he was also *weak*.

Therein lied the game.

Or rather, the lesson.

Even knowing all of this didn't help Dino to stop struggling. It didn't stop him from fighting back against the attack, despite knowing that if he just blacked out, if the men could see they had done their job, that it would all come to an end. That was all Ben wanted to do.

Teach Dino that eventually, he would get what he wanted. That Dino would always be under Ben's thumb in some way, either by manipulation, force, or both.

No, Dino still fought.

Held down.

Battered.

Probably swollen.

Definitely bloodied.

The men never said a word. Not even when Dino got an arm free and landed three solid hits of his own, one of which caused his knuckle to snap in the most painful way—either broken or dislocated, he wasn't sure.

It wouldn't be the first fucking time.

It was only when a scream echoed throughout the alleyway did the beating stop. At first, Dino wasn't sure he'd heard the sound correctly, given that blood was rushing so hard in his ears that all he could hear was the pumping of his own heart. His damn vision was too fucked up to see properly, even when he tried looking around.

He didn't realize the men were backing off until one last kick slammed into the left side of his rib cage and then it all ... stopped.

Dino blinked up at the blue sky, his head feeling like it was swimming. Even still, he tried pushing up from the ground, but the dizziness was worse like that, and he only managed to fall back down.

Grunting out his pain at the movement, he struggled to keep his eyes open.

Panic surrounded him.

Not his own, no … someone else's.

He could hear her crying in the background of the blackness starting to seep into his consciousness.

It wouldn't be long now and the abyss would be there, waiting.

It almost felt like an old friend considering how much time he'd spent with it over the course of his life.

"Dino! Oh, my God, Dino!"

That voice …

He knew that voice.

He liked that voice.

Dino thought he might have been smiling, but he quickly realized he wasn't seeing blue tinged with black any longer, but rather, a grueling streak of red oozing down to the pavement.

Blood from his mouth, he thought.

He hated blood in his mouth.

"Dino … Here, let me get you on your back."

Soft hands roved over his most tender spots.

He barely felt the pain at all.

Somehow, his vision cleared just enough for him to put the familiar face to that sweet voice.

Karen.

Fear stared back at him.

Confusion and pain.

This was *exactly* why she didn't need to be mixed up with him.

This was *exactly* why she was so much better than him.

This was *exactly* what he didn't want her knowing.

He should have told her he was sorry.

Instead, he said, "Don't call the cops."

That was more important.

For now.

CHAPTER 14

"HOLY shit—he needs a hospital!"

"I'm well aware of that," Karen snapped, her patience running thin.

Dino, drifting in and out of consciousness as he was shuffled from the ground to something else, had only caught bits and pieces of the conversation.

He didn't think he could bring back a time from his memories when he had ever heard Karen as irritated and upset as she was in that moment. And God knew he'd pissed her off a couple of times.

"He said no cops," Karen said quieter, "and the hospital will report the attack, which means—"

"Cops, yeah. I got it."

Dino groaned low when he was shifted again and his back hit something soft. It should have felt good, but the abrupt movement only caused him a hellish pain in his side.

His rib was cracked or broken.

Each breath *hurt*.

He recognized that second voice, though.

The cook.

Dino wasn't the jealous type, but he'd noticed that Karen talked to the guy who worked the kitchen a lot. The two were always laughing and going on like there was some secret they shared.

He didn't own Karen, and he didn't put titles on their strange relationship.

He didn't have any right to tell her not to enjoy someone

else's company.

That didn't mean he had to like it.

He certainly didn't want her being with someone else. Not while she was with him, anyway. Well, truth be told, he didn't want her being with someone else even if she *wasn't* with him. He just wasn't ready to deal with those feelings yet.

Although in his current situation, it wasn't exactly like he could just say something.

Dino could feel his consciousness floating away again as the conversation turned to something far worse. Something he didn't want Karen involved in at all.

"Is this because of his connections?" the cook asked.

"His *connections?*"

"Yeah—Dino's connected, you know. Everybody *knows* it, we just don't *say* it, Karen. You get to see enough shit when you work around Dino for long enough. People in suits, guns sitting on the table, or you overhear things. You learn not to pay attention, or forget what you *do* see. That's how it works."

"Connected?"

"I know you're not from Chicago and all, but come on. You don't know what that means?"

"Obviously not," Karen said shortly. "Stop being an asshole."

Just before the door slammed—the car door, likely—Dino heard the cook say, "The mob. He's connected to the mob."

Fuck.

Not that it mattered in that moment.

Dino passed out again.

The next time Dino woke up, he wasn't as fucked up as he had been. It took him a few blinks and one failed, shitty attempt to roll over before he remembered exactly what had happened that was causing the pain to ricochet through his entire body.

Letting out a slow breath, Dino forced his weight to his one side, the one that hurt less than the other, and stood up out of the bed. Pressing the heel of his palm to his throbbing temple, helped to relieve a bit of the pain, but barely. If anything, now his face hurt because he'd touched a part of it.

Wonderful.

He looked out the window, noting the light filtering in between the shades and how it danced across the floor.

Morning light, maybe?

Dino couldn't be sure.

Mindful of the pain in his ribs, Dino took careful steps, leaving the bedroom behind as he came out in the open of Karen's apartment. He wasn't surprised to be there, though he was surprised that she hadn't caved and taken him to a hospital somewhere through the night. He'd woken up on and off throughout the night to find Karen at his side each time, her soothing voice assuring him he was fine to sleep ... and *safe*.

Almost like she knew.

Maybe she did.

Dino leaned in the entryway of the kitchen that separated the dining space from the small living room. The apartment didn't have hallways, and it wasn't like it was big enough for him to hide inside.

He found Karen sitting in a large chair that seemed to swallow her whole, next to the one window in the living room that overlooked Wicker Street. She barely reacted to his presence, but he could see in the way her gaze dropped ever so slightly that she knew he was awake, and just a few feet away.

Dino counted the seconds—too many seconds—that it took for Karen to finally speak.

"Jeremy helped me to get you here. He won't say anything, so don't worry about it."

The cook, she meant.

Dino's jealousy flared to life again, and he couldn't help himself when he asked, "Did he drive?"

"No, I did."

"So he doesn't *know* where you live?"

"What does that even matter? I needed help to get you inside. Did you want me to leave you on the damn pavement since you made it perfectly clear I *wasn't* allowed to call the cops, Dino?"

"That's not what I mean." Dino glanced at the door, noting it was locked. Jeremy obviously wasn't in the apartment now, and that meant good things. "Has he been here before?"

Karen's brow furrowed. "What?"

"Jeremy—has he been here before?"

"No."

Dino did smile at that, pleased. "Good."

"Are you ... back up, did you just *smile* about that?"

Why lie?

"I did. I like that. I don't want other men being here or with you. Why would I be happy if that were the case?"

Karen stared at him for a long while, taking him in like she was seeing him for the first time all over again. "I'm not with other men, Dino."

"Good."

He didn't have to kill anyone.

That was good for all sides.

"And Jeremy is *gay*."

Oh.

Well, then.

"I didn't know that," he said.

"Seems there's a lot between the two of us that we don't know," Karen replied.

Yeah, there it was.

Dino waited her out, and thankfully, she didn't make him wait very long.

"Seems Dino DeLuca is a pretty powerful name in Chicago," she said quietly.

Dino chose his words carefully, knowing they mattered to her. "DeLuca, not me."

"Is it really that different?"

"I think so," he said honestly.

"I looked you up."

That did surprise Dino.

Especially the way she had said it so offhandedly, like it didn't even make a difference to her.

"Find anything interesting?"

Karen smiled, but it fell from her face just as fast. "A lot from when you were younger."

Dino cleared his throat, leaning against the wall but making sure to keep pressure of his bruised side and injured ribs. It would heal in time—it always did. "A lot more happened to the DeLucas when I was a teenager."

"Like your mother and father being killed?"

"Like that," he agreed. "My father turned informant for the cops. I thought it was because he wanted a better life—a *clean* life."

Karen turned slightly in the chair, giving him a better view of her profile. "Away from the … mob?"

She said 'mob' as though it were a foreign word she didn't understand.

Dino supposed she probably didn't.

Those on the outside looking in really couldn't begin to understand what the mafia was really like. They could only guess and draw their own conclusions based on the information given in the media, on the Internet, or wherever else they could find it.

It was *not* the same as living it.

It was not the same as being *inside* the mob.

"That's what I thought," Dino said, "but it was after he was dead that I realized he wanted to keep the rest of us away from it all. If only because he was just one man in a sea of men who cared nothing for the rest of them, and he didn't want us to get lost in it like he had."

"You don't sound sure."

Dino shrugged, though the action hurt a great deal to do it. "I'd got myself mixed up in family business pretty young—my dad was one of the few that tried pushing me away. It took me a decade after his death to realize he was just pushing me away from the monsters he grew up with. By that time, it was already too late."

He'd always assumed his father just didn't want him in the Outfit at all. It was only after an argument with Ben did Dino learn that his uncle's treatment of his family was not limited to the DeLuca siblings. Ben and Joseph had suffered the same handling and manipulation from their own father growing up, and then when he died, Ben had turned his anger on his younger brother.

Dino's father was probably trying to keep his sons safe from it all.

And when his plans failed, he'd gone to the officials, looking for another way out.

Not for him—for his *boys*.

It all ended rather terribly, given Ben pulled the trigger for the bullet that put Joseph in the ground, and he was left with the little people Joseph was trying to protect.

Funny how that worked.

"Why didn't you tell me about it?" Karen asked, drawing Dino from his thoughts.

"There's nothing to tell."

Karen just stared at him, sadness in her eyes and disbelief coloring her expression.

On this, he would never, ever budge.

Not with her.

"You don't need to know," Dino continued quieter, "because I don't want you to."

It was as simple as that.

She could take it or leave it.

"But are you *in* it?" she asked. "Is that why you disappear sometimes or you don't call? Is that why I've never been to your place and you park three blocks away from my apartment?"

"Does it matter?"

"Is that why you were attacked last night?"

She was fucking relentless.

Dino gave her credit where it was due.

He still refused to budge.

Maybe someday, she would understand.

This was not a hell she needed to be introduced to.

His life, aside from her, was not *normal*.

She deserved normal, happy things.

The worst part?

Dino knew he couldn't ever give Karen normal or happy.

Not entirely.

It was why he kept calling himself selfish where his involvement with her was concerned. It was yet *another* reminder that eventually, they were going to have to end whatever they were together because it would *never* go beyond the four walls of her apartment.

They couldn't *be* something because he wouldn't put her in a position to be somehow used against him, simply because he cared.

Simply because a part of him—the part that was hidden from everyone else—cared for her.

He didn't know how that had happened.

That *care* thing.

It probably started that day he met her in the cemetery when she picked him out in her day simply to make him smile. Maybe it was when she admitted that even after he rejected her, and purposefully avoided seeing her, she had still gone to his mother's grave to keep his private tradition. Or maybe it was when Karen just let him be close, or push her away, and she never really asked *why*.

She never told him not to come back.

She never hurt him.

She always smiled with him.

It was a great many little reasons that he could say he *cared* and know it was right.

That didn't mean he was going to tell her.

What if he gave it to her, and then he had to take it away?

That seemed unfair.

Cruel, even.

"Sometimes I'm not who I seem," Dino finally said, bringing Karen's attention back to him for the moment. "Sometimes shit happens and it reminds me that I have no business being here with you, no matter what I'm trying to tell myself. But I'm still here, and I keep coming back. You don't tell me to go, after all, so why wouldn't I stay when you haven't given me a reason to go?"

Karen didn't reply.

Dino didn't really need her to.

"What I said before still stands—you tell me to go, and I will."

Karen sighed, looking back out the window with what seemed like the weight of the world resting on her shoulders. "But you're not going to let me in beyond that, are you?"

She didn't seem to understand him.

"Why does it matter, Karen?"

"I—"

"You've already got the parts that *matter*."

The rest never would.

CHAPTER 15

"DINO."

He could barely move, his body feeling as though a hundred-pound weight rested on top of his back, pinning him to a floor.

A wet floor.

His fingers were able to sink into the floor beneath his body, making claw-like marks in the damp dirt.

"Dino."

Each movement was a little more painful than the last, his chest aching with every breath. He couldn't remember, though he tried like hell to bring the events back, how he got in this place. This awful, dank place.

Again.

She's just a girl, he remembered saying.

And with that single thought, it all came flying back like a wrecking ball straight to his brain, a force so destructive he had no chance to get out of the way.

She's just a girl.

Ben had laughed, struck him again, broke another bone, and promised *death*.

She's just a girl.

A girl that had caught Dino's eye—the first girl to see there was something beyond the teenager in the corner who didn't like to talk a lot. First it was just quiet chats in the hallways of the Trentini mansion, and then it moved on to bowls of soft ice-cream in the backseat of his car.

She had a pretty laugh, like the twinkling of wind chimes.

She wasn't *just* a girl.

But because he had known Ben would never approve, because he didn't want her to get in trouble because he liked her, Dino lied.

She's just a girl.

She liked to drive fast, and had the speeding tickets to prove it, though her father almost always laughed them off. Nobody thought twice about the accident—no one ever thought she'd have made that turn *if only* ...

If only she hadn't been *just something* to Dino.

And that's why he found himself there ... bleeding and unable to call out, to even beg for help. That's why his clothes were soaked in sweat and blood, and the bottom of his pants were stained with mud and vomit.

In that basement of a worn-down house Ben DeLuca grew up in, Dino could live, die, or *learn*.

Learn that he didn't get to choose.

Learn that he couldn't take what wasn't given.

Learn that he was still weak.

"Dino!"

She died on a turnpike, going fifteen over the speed limit because her breaks had been cut, while he learned from his mistake.

She'd been the mistake.

Him *caring* for her had been the mistake.

Dino never got to apologize.

At least not to her.

At her funeral, he'd stood back from the mourners, separated from the crowd because he didn't belong with them.

Ben had been right at his side the whole time.

"Look at what your selfishness caused, Dino," his uncle had said. "Look at the heartbreak they feel because of you."

"I'm sorry," he'd managed to mumble.

He'd said it only because that's what Ben had wanted.

More so, he'd said it because he knew Ben was right.

"*Dino!*"

Finally—*finally*—he saw a blackness begin to saturate the edges of the memory, promising to take it away soon and drag him back from the hell he lived in every time he closed his eyes. There was always a small part of him that held onto the memories, like a punishment of sort, because he absolutely believed that he deserved to live inside them forever.

It was his life, after all.

He should own it.

"Jesus, Dino!"

It was only the frantic panic in Karen's voice that made his eyes peel open to see the darkness of the bedroom staring back at him. His heart beat hard in his chest, sending heat and fear spinning through his bloodstream.

But he was *awake.*

Dino took a breath, and then another.

He blinked up at the ceiling as Karen leaned over him to turn the bedside lamp on, illuminating her worried face looking down at him.

"You feel like you're made of rocks," she muttered.

Her hand slid up his shaking arm, then down to his clenched fist, and skipped over the tautness of his stomach, and more carefully up to his chest. She rubbed the hardness settling in his muscles, as if willing the stress and pain away with her movements. It helped a bit, but not entirely.

Silently, she placed her palm over his racing heart, and he soaked that feeling in for a moment.

Just her hand over his heart.

Calming him.

"Bad dream," Dino said at her questioning stare.

Karen nodded slowly. "I got that."

He almost wanted to feel embarrassed, given what he knew about how he could act in the midst of his nightmares. Sometimes he talked a lot, other times he thrashed about, and drenched the bedsheets in sweat.

It was why he fought sleep as much as he could.

He'd thought he'd be okay with Karen—he had been before.

"It happens a lot?" she asked.

It came off like a question, as though he had some control in whether or not he wanted to answer, but just by the look on her face, he could tell she had already drawn her own conclusions. That was fine, because he figured it was probably obvious, given his odd nature about certain things, especially sleep.

She'd mentioned on more than one occasion that he didn't sleep nearly enough.

"'A lot' would imply I get a break from it," Dino settled on saying.

Karen winced, but she didn't try to hide it from him. "Have you ever thought about talking to someone for it?"

Dino shifted higher on the bed until his back was resting against the headboard, and used his arms as a pillow. Karen mimicked his position, albeit she didn't move far from his side. He stayed quiet for a long while, considering how exactly he wanted to answer her question. She didn't mean anything bad by it, he was sure of that fact, but it still didn't sit right with him.

"I don't talk about it with myself; I'm not about to go to someone else," he said.

"Ever?"

"No."

"Why?" she pressed gently.

Dino sighed heavily, scrubbing a hand down his bruised face. "A lot of reasons. None I'm particularly willing to share."

He was well aware he sounded like an asshole in that moment. He wouldn't blame Karen a bit, had she demanded he get the hell out of her bed *and* her life. However, like she always did, she managed to surprise him.

"What about the … other stuff?"

Dino's brow furrowed. "I don't know what you mean."

Karen fingered the hem of the sheets pooled at her waist, her gaze firmly stuck on her fiddling. Rarely had he seen her act nervous, but that action spoke entirely of unease. Dino didn't know why; he'd never given her a reason to be nervous with him, or he didn't *think* he had.

"Come on, Dino. It's one thing to shut down because you don't want to deal, it's another to shut *off* because you can't deal."

Dino didn't reply because he didn't want to repeat himself.

Karen didn't seem to mind. "If you don't want to talk to a professional about your issues or the dreams because … *whatever* … that's fine. Not understandable, but fine."

"There's nothing to talk about, Karen."

"There is."

"Nothing I'm willing to share."

"You don't have to share anything to admit you're depressed, Dino."

She could have slapped him, and he was sure it would have felt better than those words.

"I'm not—"

"Everything about you screams differently," Karen interrupted before he could deny her statement. "The way you act, how you see yourself, and the way you go about life like you're constantly closed off. It's the only thing that makes sense."

Dino wasn't willing to delve into that topic very far. "And you think I should talk to someone about it."

"I asked if you considered it."

"No."

"Would you—"

"No," Dino interjected firmly.

Karen pursed her lips, staring up at the ceiling as if she wished it would swallow her whole. "Okay."

That was it.

That was all she said about it.

As quick as the conversation had come on, it seemed like Karen was over it. Without a word, she leaned over Dino, turned the lamp off, and then settled into the bed, tucking herself back under the blankets.

For a long while, Dino sat where he was, never moving and staring at the dark wall across from him.

He knew she had a point.

The majority of his life had been spent in the belief that he was disposable.

Forgettable, even.

Worthless.

It was hard to believe anything else, when that was all he'd ever been told and shown.

But it *was* a place he understood—somewhere he felt comfortable.

It was only with Karen that he didn't feel so entirely disposable, forgettable, or worthless. She'd never treated him like he was a passing moment in her life, one that she could toss away without care, and not think about again.

Not once.

It was exactly why he kept coming back even though he was constantly reminded she was not one of the things given to him, she was something he had taken himself.

"Dino?" Karen asked in the darkness.

"Hmm?"

"Who is Julia?"

Dino stiffened, feeling a familiar spike of dread drive hard into the base of his spine. "Why?"

"Curious."

He was pretty sure he knew exactly why she was asking him about Julia. His dream that she'd woken him up from had been about her—he'd probably talked in his sleep and mentioned her name.

"There's nothing to know," Dino said quietly.

"Nothing at all?"

"Not now."

"Oh," Karen whispered, her back still turned to him. "It didn't really sound like nothing, though."

Dino wished his throat didn't feel so goddamn tight. He wished he had the right words to fend off Karen's questions without his asshole nature showing itself again. He wished he was better at this whole thing.

For her, he wished he was just *better*.

"She was someone that wasn't given to me, so she was taken away," Dino said.

He didn't need to peer down at Karen's profile to know she was probably confused as hell over his vague explanation of Julia Trentini.

It was the best he could offer.

It was the only thing that had ever been explained to him, after all.

Then, almost too quiet for Dino to hear, Karen asked, "Well, did you *love* her?"

His answer was immediate and honest. "No."

He certainly cared for Julia, but he hadn't the first clue what something like love even felt like back then, let alone now. He was sure, had he been given the chance, he would have learned what love was with her, but that wasn't the case.

Still, he'd heard that hesitance in Karen's question.

Like she'd expected a different answer from him, one that might explain his behaviors and oddities away.

He heard her *fear*.

And then he heard it again.

"Are you sure?" Karen pressed on.

"Karen."

She didn't turn in the bed, never mind responding with words.

Dino stared down at her through the darkness, wondering why she had that hitch in her words, or why she would feel like she would need to ask him that at all. Or follow it up by asking *again*.

"Karen," Dino said a second time, firmer.

Sighing, she turned to her back, her gaze drawn down. "What?"

That fear he heard in her voice—he knew what it was.

Somewhere inside, he understood she was worried that he wasn't *all here* with her because he was *scattered* somewhere else with someone that wasn't her.

He got that.

"I'm here," he told her.

Karen's gaze didn't lift to seek his out, she stayed like she was, stiff like a board beside him with her arms crossed under the blankets. "I'm aware you're here, Dino."

"Are you?"

"I know what you mean, okay. Let's go to bed. It's late."

No, not now.

He definitely wasn't going to let her sleep now.

CHAPTER 16

"HEY, listen," Dino said, shifting a bit to face Karen.

It didn't matter, as it seemed like she wasn't interested in hearing what he had to say, instead turning back to her side. The action was clear to him. She'd turned her back; she wasn't open to talk anymore.

Dino wasn't having it.

"Karen, come here."

Her cold shoulder burned, but the silence was deafening.

It cut like a fucking razor blade straight through his skin and down to his black heart.

Being injured like he was, Dino didn't need to be throwing his weight around or moving all that much for that matter, but that didn't make a difference to him in that moment. Right then, all he wanted was for Karen to actually *hear* what he wanted to say to her.

That was important to him.

It would be important *for* her, too.

"I'm not asking again," Dino said.

Actually, it was more like a warning.

One she ignored entirely.

Sitting up fully, Dino grabbed Karen's blankets and pulled them away, ignoring her cry of indignation when the cool air of the room hit her bare legs and barely dressed body. She only ever wore oversized T-shirts, or tank tops and boy shorts to bed—tonight was no exception.

Turning to glare at him, Dino let her attitude bounce right off.

He quickly slid an arm—ignoring the pain shooting through

his ribs—under her body, pulling her toward him at the same time he rolled over. He clenched his teeth, letting out a soft grunt at the sharp ache settling in his side as he got her rolled to her back, and he rested overtop her angry form.

Arms crossed, she still glared.

Dino settled in, elbows on either side of her body and comfortable where he was.

At least for the moment.

"I'm here," he told her again.

Karen frowned. "You already said that."

"With you."

"I'm aware, Dino."

"Then maybe you should start figuring out what that really means, huh?"

Karen looked less than impressed by his statement. "Maybe if you talked a little more about things, I could—"

"I'm not a talker. I don't *talk*."

"No, you stew. You live in silence—in your head. You don't let me in *there*, either. I don't know what you want me to think, Dino."

He propped his chin in his hand, contemplating her anger and how she verbalized it.

"I want you to think that I'm here, Karen."

"You keep saying that!"

"Because it matters. It's important," he murmured.

Karen rolled her eyes.

"And," Dino added quieter, "this is the only place where I am here."

She softened ... a bit.

It wasn't quite enough for Dino, though.

"There's no one else," he said. "Hasn't been for a *long* time."

"How long?" Karen asked after a long stretch of silence.

"For something like this? A decade."

"What about something not like this?"

Dino had to think about that one. "A while—long before you."

Karen's anger slowly began to dissipate, and eventually her tight, crossed arms relaxed to lay out at her sides. She still wasn't looking at him, but it was something.

He would take it.

"I worry about you," Karen said, her brow knitting together while her fingers traced the veins in his arm. "I sometimes think you could be happy if—"

"I'm happy."

He'd interrupted her statement only because he knew his words were the truth. With Karen, he *was* happy. Or as happy as he was going to get. It was not something he took for granted, regardless of what Karen might think, because he knew how fleeting and easily taken happiness really was. There were monsters in his life that made it a game to make sure he was perpetually *un*happy.

"Happi*er*," she corrected, "if you'd let me in a little more."

"You don't get it," Dino said in a harsh exhale.

Karen looked up at him, sadness coloring her brown eyes. "I do."

"You don't, because if you did, you would know you're already *in*. You've been let in for a while. It's why I keep telling you I'm here. If you understood that, we wouldn't be having this conversation right now at all."

"Oh."

"Is that all you're going to say?"

"I'm not sure what else I *should* say," Karen admitted. "Maybe I keep thinking this should be normal, or something. That if I ever want to get somewhere with you, I need to expect other things."

"Things like making me talk or making me happier?"

Karen tipped her head to the side. "It sounds stupid when you say it."

"I bet."

"You know, it's not lost on me that being here is what makes you happy, Dino."

"Good," he said, finding that smile he rarely wore but always gave to her if he could. "That's the only thing that matters."

"That, and me not telling you to go."

Dino nodded. "And that."

"As long as it's enough, right?"

"For you, sure."

Karen frowned slightly. "What if I wake up one day and it's not enough? What do I do then?"

He didn't have an answer for her. Not one that she would like, or one that he liked. He struggled for an answer, and Karen didn't miss it.

"Are we just waiting that moment out?" she asked.

Dino didn't—wouldn't—say yes to that.

He was not going to agree to *that*.

"No," he said.

Karen's brow rose. "No? I'm not sure what else we're working toward, Dino."

"Not that."

He was all too aware that she was not given to him. That she was not a part of the life he wanted to keep her safe and far away from. He understood perfectly well that she would need things he couldn't give, and the *good life* was not a part of the plans he offered.

What he gave was what she got.

Late nights.

Short conversations.

Private moments.

Them.

He didn't have much else to give.

But honestly, he didn't give that to anyone else.

"Karen," Dino said, cupping her face in his hands so he could make her look at him. In the brown eyes staring back at him, he found solid ground. He didn't like to feel as though he were constantly falling, never able to stand. It was good to be grounded somewhere—with *someone*. He couldn't help that the rest of his life, barring the spots she brightened, were such a mess. "We don't have to work toward anything at all. Isn't this good?"

"I didn't say it wasn't."

"But you don't say it is, either."

Karen smiled faintly. "It is *good*, Dino. But I wonder if it could be better."

"By making me better, you mean."

"If you think you need to be."

"Not when I'm with you, sweetheart."

"Oh."

Leaning down, he captured her soft lips with his own, lingering there to hold that kiss for as long as he could. And when she sighed, pleased and happy at his surprise, he took that small opening she gave to deepen the kiss so that he had her warmth and taste on his tongue.

It took practically nothing at all for that innocent kiss to turn into something far *hotter* when Karen's lips broke away from his, her kisses dotting over his bruised jaw and then over the racing pulse point in his throat.

She was always so soft—*gentle.*

Her touches never hurt, her actions never stung.

He liked that a lot.

When he'd lived his whole life in a world where it seemed as though everyone wanted to hurt him, to find the one person who wanted to *care* for him was everything.

"Careful," she whispered against his cheek when he reached for the clothing keeping him from finding what he wanted. "Don't hurt—"

"Hush."

His demand worked; Karen quieted, a tremor working its way over her flushed skin as Dino worked to get her boy shorts down her legs and then once they were gone, pulled off her tank top, too. And yeah—it hurt a lot. His ribs ached with every movement, his injuries and wounds protesting each time he bent down to kiss her again.

But the silkiness of her skin under his hands was easier to focus on.

The way she bent into him, her back arching like a pretty bow under his touch, was far better to feel than the pain.

There and *yes, please* and *more, Dino* breathed in his ear when his fingers found her wet and hot between her thighs was a much more pleasant sound to hear.

He didn't care that the pain in his ribs took on an almost stabbing quality when he kicked his boxer-briefs off. He didn't care at all because that first thrust into her body, in the darkness with her skin glowing and his hands holding her tight, was *heaven.* Her sharp gasp echoed as her thighs fell open wider, letting him push in even fucking deeper. Her heels dug into his back, pressing and urging, while her fingernails scored into his shoulders and held so damn tight.

Tight like her pussy, he thought.

He could barely breathe when he was inside Karen.

It was a natural high, a cloudy sensation that colored up his mind and took focus in his body. A tightening sensation that curled in his gut with every thrust of his hips that demanded a little bit more while she asked to have it *a little bit harder*.

He liked that the best.

Her sweet sounds in the darkness.

Soft skin.

The slap of skin and her breath in his ear.

It made a beautiful melody, and he wasn't exactly one for music.

Except for Karen's.

She made the best kind with him.

"*God*," she mumbled.

Another shudder crawled over her skin, and Dino caught her next moan with a kiss, swallowing it whole and keeping that same frantic, frenzied pace.

He just wanted her to come.

He wanted her to come, and then he could find his own bliss, too.

Then maybe, in the morning, he could talk more.

Maybe the world wouldn't seem so black.

It was always bright with her.

Dino's hand slid up Karen's side to her throat, barely holding there before it moved higher to hold her chin and keep her looking at him as he fucked her. It got him off—seeing how her brown eyes shimmered with sin and need while she took every little bit that he gave.

"Come," he told her.

Karen swallowed hard, her response catching in her throat. The very tips of his fingers glided over her wet lips, and in a blink, she had his fingers deep in her mouth, sucking on them as a moan vibrated in the back of her throat.

"*Fuck*."

She came fast, tasting her own arousal on the same fingers he'd used to touch her with, while her head fell back and every muscle in her body clenched. He felt her teeth bite down on his fingers, and that was it for him.

The pressure building in the base of his spine released, and the pleasure raced after it as he gave one thrust, and then another before emptying himself as deep as he could manage into her clenching pussy.

Hot, wet, and tight.

Her body held him there long after he was done, as her

fingers danced up his spine, and her tongue teased along the knuckle of his index finger.

Dino's hand splayed over Karen's cheek, and he turned her face so he could look at her again. A pleased, blissed glimmer stared back in her gaze, her lips smiling in that lax way of hers that said she was happy, and tired.

She hummed under his weight, her cheek nuzzling into his palm.

"Don't ever ask me to go," Dino said, "and I'll be as happy as I need to be."

Karen nodded, kissing the pad of his thumb as it stroked the seam of her lips. "I won't—I promise."

CHAPTER 17

DINO stared at the ceiling of his bedroom, unwilling to move. Well, part of him was unwilling, the other part simply had no desire to face the day. Eventually, despite the way his body protested and his mind screamed at him to stay right where he was, Dino got up and headed for the bathroom.

He barely felt anything under the scalding hot water of the shower, and made it quick as to not waste more time than he already had. He wasn't even in the shower long enough to fog up the mirror—his mistake—so he was stuck staring at his reflection when he got out.

Depression, Karen had said.

The men in this life didn't talk about those sorts of things. And *if* by chance they did, it was almost always about someone's wife who popped one too many pills or drank a bit too much at dinner to ignore what was happening around her.

He understood that depression was more than being stuck in bed or suicidal ideation. It was also wrapped up in a person's sense of self, or even how they felt physically. Depression couldn't be summed up in a neat little bow tied around a prescription bottle, despite how too many people thought they could fix depression by doing just that.

Karen meant no harm by bringing it up.

Unfortunately, Dino couldn't get it out of his head.

It was also why, regardless of knowing he *should* take another day or two to relax as much as he could before heading back to work and showing his face, Dino forced himself out of Karen's bed, into his own, and now, to get the hell out of his apartment. He didn't want to feed into that whispering voice in the back of his head with its *what ifs*.

What if he *was* depressed?

What would that mean?

Dino wasn't willing to find out, if only because he didn't think it mattered. Feeding into the idea that he had a problem would do him no good in the lifestyle he lived. No one was out to lend him a helping hand, and if anything, something like *that* would only be another weakness to poke at. A very visible, raw wound that he couldn't protect from people like his uncle.

It didn't matter because it wouldn't make a difference.

Feeling worthless was one thing. He didn't see how being told there was a *reason* why he felt that way would make it better.

It wouldn't.

Refusing to give his reflection or thoughts anymore time that morning, he headed out of the bathroom, a towel slung around his waist and a smaller one in his hand. He ran the smaller towel through his hair as he stepped into the closet of his bedroom, pulling out one of the three-piece suits hanging on the rack.

It was only after he was dressed and tying the laces of his black dress shoes did Dino finally feel like he might be able to handle getting through the hell the day was sure to bring. While the bruising on his face had gone—he still had a bit of yellow under his right eye—the pain from the rest of his beating was still very much there.

This was how Ben's game was played.

No one ever questioned why Dino would disappear for a week—his uncle always had some excuse at the ready. Dino was, by Ben's belief, expected to come back to life when he was ready to do so with his lesson learned, and his mouth firmly *shut*.

It was never easy.

It had gotten harder and harder to do over the years.

But as Dino strolled out of his bedroom and made his way to the kitchen to grab a coffee before heading out, he was reminded of his reasons for being stuck like he was in this terrible fucking life and situation.

One of those reasons happened to be sitting at his kitchen table.

Theo worked at the table, the dismantled pieces of a handgun spread out across the wood. Piece by piece, he picked up the metal and buffed and shined, cleaning each one until they all gleamed a bright black under the kitchen light. He seemed thoroughly involved in his work, not once looking up to greet Dino as his brother made himself a coffee.

Dino thought it odd that his brother was there.

Theo rarely came around to his place. He had better things to be doing, or so he always said. It didn't help that the brothers couldn't stand to be in each other's presence for too long before they started snapping at one another about the smallest fucking thing.

Something else they could blame on Ben, honestly.

"Morning," Dino said as he took a seat at the table, opposite of Theo.

His brother didn't look up as he began reassembling the handgun. "Morning."

"I thought I told you the key you have was for emergencies only."

"Define 'emergency.' I probably have a different meaning."

Dino resisted the urge to roll his eyes. "What's up, Theo?"

Finally, Theo glanced up, his familiar brown gaze traveling over Dino's form quickly, up to his face, and then stopping on the yellowed bruise under his eye. Just like that, Theo dropped his gaze and went back to his gun as if nothing was wrong.

"I'm fine," Dino said, knowing what his brother was thinking without even needing to be told.

"Sure. Now."

"I was fine *all* week, Theo."

Theo frowned, but didn't look up. "When?"

Dino sighed heavily, putting his cup down before he scrubbed a hand over his face. "We don't have to get into the details."

"Why?"

"Because I don't want to talk about it."

"No, *why* did it happen?" Theo asked, sliding bullets back into the gun clip one at a time. The clink-clink-clink sound as the bullets filled the clip was almost soothing in a way. Dino wondered if that's why his brother found himself repeating the ritual of cleaning his gun twice, if not three times, a day. "Because how old do you have to be exactly before it's enough for you, Dino?"

Well, he was not expecting that question.

Theo might be surprised at the answer.

"If he's fucking with me, then he's leaving you alone. Right?"

Theo's head snapped up, his gaze landing on Dino once more. "*What?*"

Dino wasn't surprised that the concept—or rather, the rationalization—he offered was foreign to Theo. They weren't *friends*, and they barely liked one another. Years of being manipulated and used to hurt the other one had really taken its toll on whatever closeness the brothers might have shared when they were younger.

However, that meant very fucking little to Dino.

Theo was still his brother.

He'd look out for him, no matter what. It was the best he could do after the way they had grown up.

"It's not about what I am or am not willing to take before I say enough is enough," Dino said, his attention going to his coffee cup instead of his brother.

It was easier that way—easier to speak when he'd rather just stay quiet and let Theo draw his own conclusions. That was probably a great portion of the trouble between the two. Dino let Theo think what he wanted, and sometimes, that meant his brother thinking he was a fucking cocksucker who didn't give two shits either way.

"It's never been about that," Dino added after a beat of silence.

"Then what?" Theo asked.

"Most people in the Outfit had the luxury of choosing to be where they are. They wanted to be a part of this thing—the mafia. We were never given that choice, not really."

"I chose this," Theo said quietly.

Dino stared hard at his brother. "Do you really believe that?"

Theo didn't answer.

Dino figured his brother didn't really have to.

"This was pushed on me—on you, too—and even Lily, though I gave her a way out, at least for a little while," Dino continued on when Theo stayed silent. "And there's not a fucking soul in the Outfit who gives a single shit what goes on within the DeLuca family as long as we're making money and paying dues to the boss. That's all that ever mattered. So yeah, Theo, I'm here because I can *take* it. Because I've taken it for *years*. It's easier for me to be the fuck up—the one person in the DeLuca family that toes Ben's line of what's okay. Then, he's not coming for you."

Theo opened his mouth to say something, but Dino beat him to it.

"And he's also not going for Lily," Dino finished quieter. "You don't have to like it at all. Shit, Theo, you don't even have to *like* me, and you can blame me for whatever you want. I've been dealing with that for years, anyway. It's nothing new. But don't ever think I'm *weak* because I don't walk away. Stand in my shoes, make a different choice than the ones I'm still having to make, and then you can tell me what I am or should be doing. Got it?"

Theo wisely chose not to say anything after that.

Silently, Dino drained his coffee, wishing the caffeine had done something for him.

It hadn't.

He was still fucking exhausted.

Not that it mattered, Dino knew, as he still had to make face with his uncle later in the day for a meeting of sorts because it was tribute. No Capo could miss tribute, not unless they wanted the boss coming after them looking for their money.

If he wasn't completely drained of energy now, by the time he had to play nice with Ben DeLuca, he certainly would be.

Dino stood, walking over to the sink to rinse his cup out. He'd just put the cup in the sink when he heard Theo's words behind him.

His brother still hadn't moved from the table.

"Have you ever thought that a bullet might fix everything?"

Dino hesitated on replying, if only because he wasn't sure of the answer Theo was probing for. "It's not that simple, man."

Theo made a noise under his breath. "It *could* be."

"But it isn't." Dino turned around to find his brother was watching him. "We both know that all the Outfit needs is a reason to turn on one another—just one single reason to go for the throat. If only one family's faction thinks they have even the slightest chance to wipeout another family's faction to get themselves closer to the top—closer to the boss's seat, they're going to take that chance, no matter who it kills in the process. So I take care of one problem, but how many more is that going to leave us with then, Theo?"

"You don't know that would be what could happen."

Dino was *positive* that was exactly what would happen.

He knew the Outfit all too well.

He'd been stabbed in the back by it one too many times.

By the men who turned their cheek when a brother went after a brother, but also managed to kill the man's wife—nothing was done. By the same men who then turned their cheeks and closed their hands to the children who were left orphaned in the mess of it all. And again, by those same fucking men who pretended like they didn't *know* the pain happening behind closed doors for years.

The Outfit was not about honor and family.

It was death, blood, and power.

That's all it ever was.

That was the *only* thing the men in the Outfit wanted to achieve.

"You could think about it," his brother pressed. "I wouldn't blame you."

Dino didn't even blink. "I have thought about it. Often."

Theo looked surprised at that. "Then why not act on it?"

"We're not at the right place yet," Dino answered honestly, "and we still have a ways to go yet to be in a position where we can fight back once it all starts."

War, he meant.

Dino didn't need to spell it out for Theo. His brother would figure it out well enough on his own. War was the only thing that would happen when one of the family's highest ranking men, and the head of an Outfit faction was taken down. Should that family then be seen as weak because of their lack of standing or control in the Outfit, another family would likely come along, determined to pick up the remaining pieces, or wipe them out forever.

That's just how it went.

It was like a game.

The DeLucas were not in a good position to be taking out one of their own—it would be like cutting off a nose to spite the face.

It would do them no good.

"You let me worry about what *I'm* doing," Dino told his brother, managing a smile though he was sure it looked cold to Theo. "And you worry about what in the hell you're doing."

"Apparently what you're doing is getting the hell beaten out of you by our uncle at twenty-nine years old because you don't want to do something about it."

Theo could think that if he wanted.

That was fine by Dino. He certainly wasn't about to explain to Theo that the moment Dino decided to kill Ben, there would be an expiration date on his life, and even Theo's. Neither brother had the power behind them to make it out of a situation like that alive—it just wouldn't happen.

No, far more chips needed to fall into place first.

And should *one* of them be able to make it out alive, Dino wanted it to be Theo. He needed to make sure of that, too.

Dino strolled on past his brother, clapping an aggravated Theo on the shoulder as he passed. "Believe what you want, Theo. You always did, little brother."

Dino didn't wait around to hear Theo's response, and he let the door slam to say he didn't care if his brother even had one.

It was easier this way.

That was what he was going to keep telling himself.

CHAPTER 18

DINO was all too aware of the fact he was thirty seconds off being late for tribute when he opened the door to the downtown pizzeria owned by another Outfit Capo. Traffic had been a bitch mid-city, and he had broken just about every road law he could to get there in time.

If somebody had something to say about it, fuck them.

Ignoring the gazes falling on him as he strolled through the restaurant, heading for the large office in the back, he pulled his cell phone from his pocket, feeling it buzz. Karen's number lit up the screen.

Deja-vu, he thought as he opened her message.

Are you coming around today? Supper?

Dino hated to respond with a negative on that, but he had no other choice. He knew Theo had taken care of business while he was on the mend the week before, but that didn't mean he could afford more time away that what he'd already taken.

It was more likely that someone would notice his *distractions*.

Karen was a big distraction, no matter how much he liked it.

Still, he felt guilty as he typed back, *No.*

Then just as quickly, added, *Sorry, soon.*

Karen responded almost instantly, but Dino was already shoving his phone back into his trouser pocket, his attention on the man standing just outside the office door with a cell phone pressed to his ear. Ben didn't miss the sight of Dino strolling down the hallway, but he barely even gave his nephew a second glance before he was back to his call.

Dino didn't care, already walking into the large office where the family Capos waited to hand over the dues to their boss.

To Ben, it would be like the previous week and the beating had never happened.

That's how it always worked.

"A bit late, aren't you, Dino?"

Dino gave Walter Artino a shrug as he sat down beside the Capo. Fact was, Walter was a bastard who'd married into the Outfit and got his hooks into the DeLuca side of the family through Ben's wife's sister. But because Walter was as greedy as the rest of the men in the Outfit, and didn't mind playing dirty every once in a while to get what he wanted, he got along just fine with Ben.

That meant Dino didn't trust the fool with an inch.

He was a fucking snake.

Sometimes, Dino needed to work with Walter to get shit settled between their mutual crews and business, just to make sure things ran smoothly. It almost always ended with Walter running his mouth to Ben on just about *anything*.

So yeah, if Dino could help it, he didn't talk to the man.

Thankfully, today looked to be one of those days when he wouldn't have to offer much by way of conversation when the boss walked in followed by Ben, and then Riley Conti, the Outfit's front boss.

With the boss, underboss, and front boss in the room, the quiet chatter between the family Capos died down to nothing at all.

Terrance—never the kind of boss to sit when the rest of his men were already down, too—didn't bother to take a seat behind the large oak desk, opting to stand in front of it. Ben, as Terrance's right-hand man, took a seat on the edge of the desk, while Riley pulled a chair off to the side, looking as though he was ready to be done with tribute before it even began.

The three highest men in the Outfit couldn't be more different on the outside as far as appearances and attitudes went, yet Dino knew, on the inside, they were all the same.

One was a monster he'd been stuck under for over a decade.

Another was a bastard with a violent streak.

The other turned a cheek to the men he'd chosen to stand at his side.

Dino didn't think that, if given the chance, he could pick the lesser of evils between the three men.

And that, he knew, would be the problem.

That morning, when Theo thought it would be so easy to take out one man, forgot that the one man was a part of a three-legged stool that ran the operation they were expected to call family. Getting rid of one leg would only work if the other three went, too.

Unfortunately, now that bug was in his ear.

Dino couldn't help but hear it buzzing around in there.

"Any problems this last week?" Terrance asked his men.

Dino kept his eyes on the boss, but he didn't miss how Ben's gaze slid to him for a split second. He kept quiet, because there was no problem.

Not now.

"Good," Terrance said when no one spoke up with an issue to name. "Who has gifts for me?"

Without question, every single man in the room dug into their pockets to pull out envelops of many different sizes, depending on the man holding them. Dino's own envelop was significantly smaller than it would usually be, as instead of picking up racket payments the week before, he'd been in bed giving his cracked rib time to heal.

And fucking Karen.

That, too.

He was left with the money Theo had been given and collected over the week. It would do, if only because it was enough to cover what the boss expected to be paid from Dino, but it wouldn't go unnoticed that his tribute was significantly smaller than it usually was.

Still, Dino handed the dirty cash over without a word when Ben came around to collect. His uncle took the package with a curious glint in his eyes, then moved his hand up and down as if to test the weight of the cash.

"Low this week, Dino?" Ben asked.

"Missing a few thousand," Dino replied, uncaring of the eyes watching him around the room. "It'll be in with the next one."

"Make sure of it."

With that, Ben moved onto Walter, taking the man's offering that was even smaller than Dino's had been. That was the problem with being a secondary Capo in a family faction like the DeLucas. Dino had the majority crew, and he brought in the most money. Walter was forced to take what was left, whether he liked it or not, on the off-chance that he might someday get the control Dino had.

It was yet *another* reason why he didn't trust or like his uncle's little snake.

Walter had every reason to fuck with Dino's position in the Outfit. That was how the mob worked—men had to cut other men at the knees and then go for the throat if they wanted to move up in the family.

It would not be Dino's knees that got cut by Walter fucking Artino.

The very second Terrance had the money in his hands, he dismissed the men without bothering to linger. Dino didn't mind, and he supposed as the boss, Terrance had earned the right to sit on his ass and collect money.

After all, it wasn't easy to be at the top.

"DeLuca, stay where you are," Terrance called before Dino could even stand from his damn chair.

Dino rested back in his seat, watching as the men filed past him one by one, their conversations starting back up again. A couple nodded to him—Tommas Rossi being one, the cousin of Damian Rossi, Theo's friend—but Dino offered nothing back.

He didn't *make friends* with anyone.

Ben had beaten that lesson into him long ago.

It was the easiest rule to follow simply because Dino trusted fucking no one.

"What is it, boss?" Dino asked once the men were all gone.

Ben and Riley were busy counting money on the desk, separating the bills into three piles, their attention fully on their work.

"Your brother," Terrance said, crossing his arms.

That stopped Ben's work instantly.

"What about Theo?" Ben asked.

Terrance didn't give his underboss a response, instead, keeping his gaze on Dino. "Have you taken to mentoring him, Dino?"

Dino understood what his boss was asking him, and it was both important and significant. Especially for Theo. "Not in an official capacity."

"But you *have*."

"He's the only one willing to learn, and he's good at what he does. He's taken on just about everything I've thrown at him, and while he mouths about it, he likes it. He's on the up."

"Good," Terrance murmured. "Should you decide to take his mentoring into a more *official* capacity, I'd be willing to give him the title to go along with his button, as soon as you said he was ready for it."

A Capo, he meant.

Terrance was basically saying he was willing to give Theo his title of Capo to go along with his spot in the Outfit, as long as Dino thought his brother was capable of handling the responsibility that went along with it.

Theo was ready.

Of that, Dino was absolutely sure.

He'd go through the ropes and the rules, though, to make sure his brother got his fucking title the *right* way so that nobody could take him from him.

Ben also seemed to pick up on the hidden message in the conversation, and he didn't look particularly pleased about it. "Theo is still young—he's not ready for that sort of title, Terrance."

"And how would you know that?"

"Pardon?"

Terrance gave Ben a look. "How would you know that Theo isn't ready? You don't have him under your guidance, not in the same way Dino does."

Ben's sharp gaze turned on Dino, and for a split second, he was sure he saw a warning flashing in his uncle's eyes. For what reason, he couldn't say.

Why would Ben want to *keep* Theo from getting his status in the family?

It would do him no good, and certainly not if he wanted the brothers to move higher in the Outfit as he always claimed he did.

"He's only—"

"Let Dino decide if Theo's age is a problem to his capabilities or lack thereof," Terrance interrupted Ben without as much as a blink of an eye. Then, to Dino, he said, "Mentor him under an official capacity, make it known, and see how he does with that sort of pressure. You could use a secondary Capo to run your side of the DeLuca family—your brother is a good pick."

"He is," Dino agreed.

Clearly, Ben did not like that idea, but he was wisely choosing to stay quiet for the moment. Dino was thankful, if only because it allowed him to agree with his boss without disagreeing with his uncle.

He was not up for another fight with Ben.

Or one of the bastard's lessons.

Not when he was still healing from the last one.

"You can go," Terrance said.

Dino wasn't ready to go, yet.

Something else came to the forefront of his mind, and while he knew better than to ask while his uncle was in the room, it wasn't often that he was given time with the boss when other Capos were not around.

"Question," Dino said.

Terrance's brow lifted. "What is it?"

"Damian Rossi is still the man you send around looking for shit when you don't want people to know someone was around, right?"

The boss didn't respond. Dino didn't really need him to. He knew what the answer would be.

"Someone's been in my offices," Dino said, "and they were quiet about it."

His financial documents had been just *one* thing he noticed was missing. Since he noticed that, other things had also turned up missing as well.

One thing could be dismissed.

More was not a coincidence.

Those didn't exist in the mafia.

Terrance stared hard at Dino, an unflinching coldness gleaming in his eyes. "Are you suggesting I had Damian Rossi snooping through your business, Dino?"

"A while back, you sent him into my warehouse where I hold the fights, wanting to know if I was paying dues on the place. It's not a stretch if you think I'm trying to hide money from you."

"I don't think that."

Terrance had offered the statement so frankly that Dino didn't have a reason not to believe his boss. However, it did leave him feeling more uneasy about the whole situation. At least Terrance would have a valid reason, though that didn't mean Dino would like it any better if it *was* his boss taking his documents.

It seemed that it wasn't his boss, though.

That left him with very few options as to who it could be.

One of those people happened to be staring him right in the face, unbothered and calm as he always was, even when he was the one holding a gun to a man's head. Yet, Dino couldn't ask Ben if he was the one snooping and taking things because he didn't have any proof to be throwing out accusations like that.

Those documents could very well be the proverbial gun to Dino's head.

'*Why*' was the better question.

Why would Ben want them?

What good would it do for him to have them?

Dino was going to have to figure that out, and soon.

CHAPTER 19

"I can't just take time off whenever I feel like it," Karen argued.

Dino chuckled, amused at how she tried to sound serious, but the excitement was still ringing through her tone as clear as a bright, sunny day. "Do you want me to pull the boss card, then?"

"The *what* card?"

"The boss card. I'm the boss. It's my business. I can give whoever I want as much time off as I want, whenever the fuck I want. And why can I do that?"

Karen grumbled under her breath on the other end of the call.

"I couldn't hear that very well," Dino said.

"Because you're the boss," Karen muttered.

Knowing her, he could practically see her rolling her eyes at his teasing.

It felt good to do that, as simple of an action as it seemed. Most people had no problem lightening up with people and making jokes. It was safe to say that Dino was not *most people* and things like teasing didn't come easy to him.

Unless it was with Karen.

Things with her always seemed almost *easy*.

Dino chose not to look too far into it.

"The boss card has been pulled," Dino said gruffly, wanting to get out of his thoughts before they became a bottomless pit he couldn't crawl out of. "I will be there after supper to pick you up, make sure your shit is waiting by the door that you want to bring, and no arguments. Think of it as a vacation."

"Can I take pictures on this vacation?" Karen asked slyly.

Always the photographer.

Dino smiled to himself. "I hoped you would, actually."

"Okay."

His laughter echoed in the office long after Karen had hung up the call with a rushed 'gotta go pack.' He should have just told her that her love of photography was on the table from the beginning, where the weekend away was concerned. He doubted that she would have argued with him at all about it then.

Still, his chuckles continued as he leaned back in his chair and scrubbed a hand over his face. It was only when a throat cleared at the door did Dino's amusement fade and he was brought back to the present with a bang.

Standing with his arms crossed and a curious expression was Theo.

Not far behind his younger brother, Dino could see another guy. He was younger than Theo, and unfortunately, not someone Dino particularly liked or trusted.

Dean Artino—Walter Artino's son.

They were all a bunch of snakes slithering in the same pit together.

Ben had always liked to press upon Dino how he shouldn't play with the snakes in other peoples' families as he'd grown up, but Ben never stopped to look at the snakes within his own grass.

"What?" Dino asked sharply.

Theo shrugged like nothing was amiss. "You seem happy."

"That's a problem? I can't be happy?"

He knew damn well that he sounded harsh, and probably a little deflective. Dino didn't really have a choice but to do what he had to in order to keep people the hell out of his business at whatever cost.

Even Theo.

Especially Theo.

Dino didn't want his brother more mixed up in his mess than he had to be.

Theo was already moving on to another topic at hand, waving at the young man behind him. "Artino sent his kid over for you to look after for the day."

Dino passed Dean a look, and then went right back to his brother. "You can't do it?"

"Other shit—Ben, you know," Theo offered, saying nothing more.

Well, Dino supposed he wouldn't be getting out of the club as soon as he wanted, but he could still make it to Karen's place in lots of time like he promised. That didn't mean he was particularly happy about having to watch the Artino kid.

Besides, watch was only a euphemism for *teach*.

Apparently, Walter wanted his son in the Outfit, but he wasn't all that interested in making sure the kid understood exactly what that meant.

No, that job had suddenly fallen to Dino.

Too close, he thought, taking in Dean's disinterested expression.

He hated how it felt like Ben was getting too close to him in certain ways again, like planting someone at his side, perhaps because Theo was not good enough anymore for Ben's plans.

Especially considering Theo was Dino's understudy.

All that work Ben had put into separating the brother's was torn to shreds by one simple demand from the boss shoving them back together.

Of course, that didn't mean Dino and Theo had to like it.

"We done, or what?" Theo asked.

Sometimes, his attitude burned like acid.

Dino didn't really have to ask why, though. "Yeah—get out."

Theo left, but unfortunately, the snake stayed behind.

"Stop rushing me," Karen said, giving Dino a half-hearted glare over her shoulder. "It takes a while to get all of this packed up properly."

"I should have made rules about this."

"Do tell, Dino. What kind of rules exactly?"

Dino prided himself on the fact he wasn't a particularly stupid man. Sometimes his actions didn't always reflect that, but this time, he knew better. He was not about to take the bait Karen just offered and jump into an argument with her.

Not today.

It was supposed to be a *good* day.

"Do you need all of that equipment?" Dino carefully asked, waving at the bags Karen had set out for him to take to her car.

Karen's gaze flicked between Dino and the bags. "You said I was going to take pictures. I need my stuff, Dino."

"Yes, but *all* of it?"

Because it looked like she was bringing her whole damn studio setup.

"Well, probably not all of it," Karen admitted. "But you didn't say where we were going to, or what we would be doing there, so I have to be prepared."

"Because I'm trying to make it a surprise, sweetheart."

Karen smiled, her brown eyes twinkling with amusement.

That was really all Dino hoped to achieve by doing this for her—a smile, her happiness, and time away from the bustle of a city that seemed to be swallowing him whole every other day. Karen wanted to do normal things, like go out to dinner or take a weekend trip away. Dino had woken up that Saturday with a sudden need pressing down on his shoulders like it was the weight of the world; he wanted to do *normal* for her.

Even if it was only a weekend outside of the city in a small cabin on a lake.

It was still something.

"I don't think you'll need all of it," Dino said, "but maybe half of it won't hurt."

Karen seemed to accept that answer easily enough, and quickly went about picking through her pile of photography equipment to decide what was going, and what stayed behind. She did it carefully, weighing the pros and cons of leaving certain lenses behind, never mind picking between three cameras. Eventually, she narrowed it down to one camera, and two bags.

Dino was grateful.

She had been so involved in her work at his restaurant that she hadn't had time to indulge her love of photography as often as she used to. Dino knew that she was thankful for the job and money, because now bills and food were the last thing she had to worry about at the end of the month. He still didn't have any doubt that if offered the chance to do what she loved, Karen would take it in a heartbeat.

Really, Dino didn't blame her.

He hoped this weekend away would give her the chance to get back behind the camera, if only for a short time, and forget that the rest of world existed.

He just wanted to watch her get lost, and do the same.

It was a simple enough request, wasn't it?

Dino didn't think he was asking for much.

"Are we going to get on the road?" Karen asked, bringing Dino out of his thoughts as she came to stand in front of him. "Or are you going to keep standing there and staring at me?"

Mischief practically wafted from her.

She was so happy.

She never once questioned him about all of this, or why he was doing it, for that matter.

It was one of many things he liked a great deal about Karen. She was grateful for what he gave, and never really asked for more. She didn't push him beyond the lines in the sand he drew, even when she probably should.

"Yeah," he said after a moment, "we can get on the road."

"Good." Karen flashed him a beaming smile and slung her weekend bag over her shoulder. "Be careful with my—"

Before she could even finish that sentence, Dino leaned down and pressed a hard kiss to her mouth to shut her up. Karen's surprised squeak quickly melted away and she pushed closer to him, one of her hands wrapping around his neck and tangling into his hair to keep him in place. She wasted no time deepening the kiss as he grabbed her around the waist and held her tight.

All too soon, he was pulling away, needing to clear the sudden cloud that had fallen over his mind. Karen blinked up at him, a lazy, happy grin curving the edges of her pink lips upward.

"That was nice," she whispered. "Unexpected, but nice."

"I'll take care of your stuff," he said. "You don't have to tell me to. You know that, right?"

Karen stared up at him, silent and searching in her gaze. He had the distinct feeling that she too had caught the true meaning in his words, despite how they had sounded on the surface.

It wasn't just her stuff, but her, too.

He'd take care of her.

Without asking.

Without being told.

Because he wanted to and it felt right.

Finally, Karen nodded. "Yeah, I know, Dino."

"*Perfetto*," he murmured.

Her brow raised slightly at his casual use of Italian. It wasn't something he did often in her presence, and honestly, he didn't do it a lot in business, either. Not unless he had to, anyway.

"Say something else," Karen said. "If you can, I mean."

Dino didn't hesitate. "*Sei la mia luce.*"

"And what does that mean?"

Something incredibly important that he didn't think he had the guts to say to her in English, so he didn't. Shaking his head, Dino gave Karen a wink and stepped to the side, out of her embrace.

"Get down to the car and pop the trunk for me," he told her.

"You're seriously not going to tell me what it means?"

"Not today, sweetheart."

Karen gave him a mock scowl, but it was only a half-hearted effort. "Fine, I'm going to the car."

Dino grabbed the bags, balancing them carefully as he scooped up the apartment keys from the coffee table. He made sure to triple-check the locks before being satisfied the place was closed up tight. One couldn't be too careful.

Outside in the complex parking lot, he found Karen waiting in the car. Once he had all the bags situated in the trunk, he too slid into the car, more than ready to get the hell away for the weekend.

Even though it was her car, Karen sat in the passenger seat.

"You can drive," Dino said.

He would rather drive, but he'd let her take the wheel.

"I don't know where we're going, Dino. Remember?"

True enough.

"I could give you directions," he offered, holding the keys out to her.

Karen smiled, and shook her head. "This is *your* surprise for me. You do it the way you want."

How exactly was he supposed to argue with that?

It didn't take long at all for them to get on the road, and then the highway leading out of the city. He couldn't take her too far, certainly not out of country or even the state, if only because he had his phone turned on in case something happened over the weekend and he got called back. As much as he hoped that didn't happen, and for as much effort as he had put into taking care of things *and* people so they didn't question his absence for two or three days, it was still a very real possibility.

The drive was silent, and Dino focused on the cars ahead of him, weaving in and around other vehicles to get ahead of them as fast as possible.

He wanted to get out of the city.

He wanted to leave the Outfit behind.

At least for a short while.

Karen's hand found his on the middle console, and without a word of request, Dino weaved their fingers together, then placed their joined hands on her jean-clad thigh. There, he could stroke her leg with the side of his thumb while he drove.

The action was soothing.

He didn't really question *why* but instead, took the comfort it offered.

"You're really not going to tell me what that meant, huh?" Karen asked out of the blue.

Dino looked over at her, taking in the beautiful warmth she radiated and how her face lit up whenever he gave her his full attention.

This whole weekend would be nothing but that, he knew.

His attention on her.

Only her.

"I'm curious what it means," she pressed.

Dino still couldn't tell her.

Not yet.

Still, his mind whispered the words—the truth.

You are my light.

Because to Dino, Karen was the brightest spot in his very dark world, always lighting up the shadows that never really seemed to leave.

It seemed apt.

There were a dozen and one other things he could have said to her in Italian—things that would have been safer, that he could have repeated in English without her looking too much into it or overthinking what it all meant.

This was not the same.

And he wasn't ready to explain what it all meant.

Or rather, what it might mean for him and her.

Maybe he was a fucking coward.

"Not today," he finally said.

With a sigh—although it sounded happy, more than anything else—Karen rested back into the seat, placing her feet up on the dashboard. "You're so strange sometimes, Dino."

She kept saying that, but ...

"I don't think it makes much of a difference to you, does it?"

Karen eyed him from the side. "No, it really doesn't."

CHAPTER 20

KAREN'S eyes lit up as the trees began to clear up ahead on the dirt road. It was getting dark fast, but there was still more than enough light to see what awaited them for the weekend.

The split-level log cabin sat proudly on the edge of a lake, looking both old and comforting at the same time. It was a place Dino had purchased a while back if nothing more than for the land it offered, and the view he thought he might enjoy taking advantage of at some point.

He hadn't been wrong on both accounts.

It was private, and that would do him well this weekend with Karen.

And the view …

Well, he had the best view sitting right beside him.

Karen pulled her legs down from the dashboard and leaned forward in the seat, taking in the cabin as they came closer. She peered out the windows, her interest growing at the sight of the lake and floating barge with a small boat attached.

"This is yours?" Karen asked. "All of it?"

Dino shrugged as he pulled Karen's car to park in front of the cabin. "It is, but it's nothing compared to some of the other places around the lake. A lot of the other properties are hidden by trees or set higher on the hills."

"Nothing? Dino, this place is beautiful."

He hadn't really noticed before, as his moments spent here had only been to get away fast and then be called right back to life. He never had the time to enjoy it as much as he knew it deserved to be, never mind care for the place hands-on. He paid someone else to do that for him.

By the looks of the chimney, with gentle puffs of gray smoke popping out of the top, the groundskeeper and maid had come in and done their job on time. Dino made a mental note to include a bonus in with their checks at the end of the month.

Glancing over at Karen with a smile, he asked, "So you like it?"

"*Love* it."

"You'll probably like the inside even more."

Karen rolled her eyes and waved at the forest and lake surrounding them. "I doubt it."

"You just want to take pictures."

She didn't even deny it.

"Do you *see* this place, Dino?" Karen asked, opening her door and stepping out of the car. "It's a nature photographer's *wet dream*."

Dino cleared his throat, stepping out of the car himself and closing the door. "A *wet* dream, huh?"

Karen shot him a sly smile, promising and wicked all at the same time. "You don't know *all* of the things that turn me on."

"Yet."

She hesitated in her steps, glancing over her shoulder at him. "What?"

"I don't know them all yet. Give me time."

Karen's smile melted into a sensual grin. "We do have all weekend."

And then they'd have to go back.

Unfortunately.

Dino was already trying to figure out how fast he could get back here with Karen after they had to leave. Suddenly, the place didn't feel like just another deed with his name on it, but rather, a place where the rest of the world couldn't touch him.

If only for a time ...

"The front door should be unlocked," Dino said as he rounded the car to pop the trunk.

He was just grabbing their bags as Karen took the few steps leading up to the cabin's entrance two at a time. The entryway was made of four large tree trunks that acted as pillars, with thick logs as overhangs and forest green shingles to help the cabin blend in when looking down from up above.

Dino had only made it half way across the front yard when he heard Karen gasp loudly, then shout a happy yell. She'd left the door to the cabin wide open, and he only saw a brief peek of her back and caramel-toned hair before she was gone in a flash, probably to explore the inside of the two-level cabin.

Stepping inside the place, Dino was careful to set the bags down, and out of the way as he listened to the patter of Karen's feet upstairs. The winding staircase that led to a loft-like upper section was also made out of curved logs and split wood stained a deep chestnut. Even the fireplace, made from stones that had been pulled from the ground when the previous owner dug out what would be the basement, had been meticulously designed, giving it a hand-crafted and beautiful feel.

The walls, exposed rafters, and even the crown-molding and baseboards were all made with the same hand-crafted beauty, and all were stained with that same chestnut color, making the place feel both warm and natural.

Like the earth, Dino thought.

A person couldn't be closer to nature than a cabin in the woods.

The one thing that really made the cabin stand out were the large floor-to-ceiling windows that covered one entire back wall, tapering off into a point once the glass reached the sloped roof. In the day, the place didn't need much light because those windows provided far more than enough all on their own.

"Dino!"

"Yes?"

Karen appeared above his head, her hair blowing out around her face as she leaned precariously over the wooden railing. "The bed up here is made out of logs!"

Her simple joy over something so random made his chest tight while a warmth spread fast from his fingertips through to the rest of his body. He didn't quite understand *why*, but he liked it a lot. He liked that he could make her smile, and that all the little details that the place had to offer were the kinds of things that someone like Karen could appreciate.

He'd never brought someone here before.

She was the first, and would probably be the last.

Still, Dino knew, Karen was exactly the kind of person who

would understand the worth and beauty that went into each and every inch of the cabin. Even *he* hadn't fully understood the work and love it took to build the place at first—he'd only seen rooms, logs, and a lake. But he did know now.

Dino chuckled. "They all are. The guy who built the place liked to work with his hands. Everything from the floors to the kitchen cabinets came from the trees he cleared off the lot to build the place."

"Really?"

He nodded.

Karen looked around again. "Why did he sell it?"

That, Dino didn't have an answer for. Not a good one, anyway.

"He just said it was time—I happened to be the lucky fucker who gave the right bid."

"Huh," she said, more to herself than him.

Then, she was gone again, pushing away from the railing and disappearing from his view. Dino didn't have to wait for very long before she appeared again, bouncing down the stairs, her smile growing wider with each step.

Before long, she was standing in front of him, pushing up to her tip toes, and kissing him sweetly.

Dino froze, not expecting the kiss. "What was that for?"

"Being you."

"Being *me*."

Karen kissed him again, harder and longer, whispering as she pulled away, "Because you're wonderful, Dino."

"I think you have you and I mixed up," he said quietly.

"No, I think you just don't see yourself clearly."

Well, he wasn't going to argue with her.

It was up to Karen whether or not she believed Dino was worth keeping around, or just worthless.

He didn't get a say in that at all.

Dino sat on the edge of the dock, watching the floating barge move further and further away from his spot. Given it was tied to the dock, it would only go as far as the rope would allow, and then he would just have to pull it back and tie it again.

The sight was relaxing, so much so that he barely realized the sun had started to peek over the horizon again, signaling morning was fast approaching.

It would be their second to last day at the cabin, unfortunately. Monday, bright and early—they would need to head back for the city. Dino didn't quite realize how much he would want to stay right where he was, with Karen and a quiet forest, rather than Chicago.

Sighing, he let his leg drop off the dock and leaned back, using his hands to keep him upright. He surveyed the peaceful lake, taking in the two other properties he could see from his position on the other side of the pond. It was unlikely whoever owned the places—if they were even home—could see his position without binoculars. It had been the one sense of relief he had when Karen had wanted to take the boat out the day before.

It wasn't like Dino could refuse her.

It was a weekend for her, after all.

Well, for *them*.

Frankly, Dino had made a far greater effort to ensure Karen was happy and had all the time in the world to do whatever she wanted the past two days and evenings. And she *had* gotten to do whatever she asked of him, from taking the boat out, hiking through the trails, taking pictures of this or that, and then more of *that* again.

He never complained.

He didn't have a reason to.

Seeing her beam with every 'yes' he gave only made him feel lighter.

Why wouldn't he want to feel lighter when all he ever seemed to feel on a good day was weighed down?

Peering out at the lake once more, Dino was reminded that this was really the first time he had taken any sort of moment to fully enjoy what this place had to offer. Previously when he'd come down, he hadn't even bothered to ask the groundskeeper to pull the sheets off the furniture. Dino was lucky if he bothered to drag himself beyond the wood shed.

Karen hadn't given him much of a choice this time, and he hadn't minded following along to feed her whims about whatever adventure she wanted to try.

He'd be back soon, he knew.

With Karen, of course.

Dino grabbed his coffee cup sitting beside him on the dock and lifted it for a sip, taking in the lukewarm, bitter liquid. He'd been up before dawn—not because he couldn't sleep, as he had slept quite well—and quickly got bored with wandering the house.

He thought it would be selfish to wake Karen from her dreams because he couldn't amuse himself while he was alone.

Strange as that is, he thought.

Dino had never minded *being* alone before, and certainly had no problem with keeping himself company. Yet, whenever he was with Karen, his entire outlook seemed to change and the very last thing he wanted was to be left to his own devices. She was far more interesting, anyway.

The gentle sound of a camera's shutter going *click-click-click* - behind him had Dino resting his cup back to the dock as he glanced over his shoulder. He found Karen standing at the very end of the dock, her camera raised and shielding most of her face as she took another round of shots. For a second, he thought she was taking pictures of the lake.

It took him far too long to realize she was actually taking pictures of *him*.

"I'm not a very good subject," Dino said.

He didn't smile very often, and he didn't perform.

Karen never lowered the camera as she came closer. "You're a perfect subject—haunted, alive, beautiful, and *real*. What more could I ask for?"

Dino swallowed the thickness building in his throat, and turned back to face the lake. He could still hear Karen's camera clicking wildly as she continued taking his picture. He was so accustomed to staying *out* of the limelight that even something like a photograph felt strange.

Still, he let her take the pictures.

Whatever made her happy.

Soon, Karen was at his side, her camera lowered as she too stared out over the lake. He took her in from the corners of his eyes, the swell of her hips under tiny, khaki shorts and the dip in her waste accentuated by the crop-top with a fringe bottom. She was always so professional at the restaurant, dressing for her job, the establishment, and the position she carried. Even when she was home alone, she dressed comfortably, but modestly.

Here, Dino had gotten to see a bit more of Karen in a different element.

He liked to think it was probably an element she was more comfortable in.

"I'm going to miss it here," she said.

Dino nodded his agreement. "But we'll come back."

"Yeah?"

"As soon as I can get away."

Karen didn't question him on what he had to get away from, and he was grateful. Without warning, her hand fell to the nape of his neck, her fingers threading through his hair. Subconsciously, Dino found himself leaning into her touch, his head resting against her thigh as her fingers ran over his scalp with tender strokes.

"Could have woke me up," she said softly.

Dino shook his head. "I was up too early to be waking you up, too."

Karen laughed. "I do like to sleep in."

"Come here." Dino grabbed Karen around the waist and pulled her giggling self into his lap, making the dock rock from the movement. Once she was situated in his lap, her camera forgotten to the dock as she straddled him with her hands cupping his jaw and his hands grasping firmly to her waist, he felt lighter again. Clear in the head, calm in his heart, and content in his soul.

A soul that was usually so dark—battered, blackened, and wasted—was reborn with her.

He was a little amazed by that, honestly.

"Promise that's all it was," Karen said.

Dino understood what she was asking—did a nightmare wake him up?

"I'm good," he promised.

She smiled, then leaned forward and pressed her soft lips to his. It only took a slight shift of her hips on top of his groin, her lips parting to let his tongue dive in deeper, seeking out the heat and sweetness of her mouth, and the press of her hands against his chest, and Dino was falling backwards to the dock.

Karen laughed above him, bending down to kiss him again.

Silently, he offered her his hands, and she met his palms with her own without question. Their fingers weaved together, tangled tightly and she didn't let go.

"I almost don't want to go back," Karen said. "You spoiled me all weekend."

He had—late nights, later mornings, and he'd taken advantage of each one by seeing just how loudly Karen could scream his name in a forest where no one could hear her. On her knees, her back, or hell, standing up against a wall.

Fun and games, he knew.

It certainly had been fun.

But every game came to an end, eventually.

"We'll be back," he promised again.

Maybe …

Maybe next time, they wouldn't have to leave.

CHAPTER
21

DINO swung the axe again, the heavy tool cutting fast through the air before slicing through the block of wood with ease. There was something relaxing about chopping wood.

It certainly wasn't that he and Karen needed wood for heat in the cabin. The weather was warm enough without the fireplace being put to use, but Karen had liked the sight and smell of it in the evening.

Dino had gone out to the wood shed to bring in a handful of blocks—all they would need for their last night at the place—and noticed how the pile of split wood was getting a bit low. There was still lots of wood, it just wasn't bucked up and ready for the fireplace.

Of course, Dino hadn't really needed to grab the old axe from the corner of the shed and get to work on splitting wood. He paid a guy to do all of that and a lot more where the property was concerned, but he was there, there was time, it was *his* place, so why not help while he could?

Plus, the guy who looked after the place was in his mid-fifties. The man never complained, and he always took great care of the property just how Dino asked for him to, including keeping it warmed in the winter, which meant a drive out to the property at least once a day, if no one was living in the cabin, just to keep the fireplace full.

And despite the fact they hadn't actually needed the fireplace or the wood during their weekend visit to the property, Dino had been pleased to see there actually was enough split wood for them to use should they need to.

That meant his guy was doing his job.

Still, Dino had nothing better to do for a while, Karen was entertaining herself, and so he grabbed the axe, ready to work.

He'd never found work quite this relaxing.

Before he knew it, Dino had split a quarter of the cord of wood. His T-shirt had been hindering the force of his swing, so it now rested over top of the wood pile, forgotten. A bead of sweat trickled down his spine, reminding him that as relaxing as this was, it was still a goddamn workout.

Another five or so swings later, and Dino was sure he had heard the screen door close—the side exit of the cabin. He couldn't see it from his position to check, so he kept working. Grabbing another large block of wood, he set it up properly in front of him, grabbed the axe by the base with his left hand and the middle with his right, and swung. The block snapped into three pieces.

The soft clearing of a throat stopped him from grabbing another bock. Dino used his previously discarded shirt to wipe his brow and chest before tossing it away again, and turning to face Karen.

She wasn't exactly looking at him—well, not his face.

Her gaze traveled down the length of his body, lingering on his chest and then lower, stopping for a long while at the hard cut V of his groin where his pants hung low around his waist. Her tongue peeked out to wet her lips before disappearing back inside her mouth just as quickly.

Karen's gaze finally made its way back up to Dino's face, and he cocked a brow at her, smug and silently questioning. Her cheeks turned the sweetest shade of pink he had ever seen in his life.

"Find something you like?" he asked.

Karen shifted on her feet, throwing a glance over her shoulder. "I wondered what was taking you so long."

"That doesn't answer my question, sweetheart."

"You already know I like it, Dino."

"So say it."

Karen's sheepish gaze turned almost playful. "I didn't know you could chop wood. You're kind of a pretty, city boy, aren't you?"

Dino scoffed. "*Pretty*, city boy?"

"Kind of."

"I can also fix just about anything under the hood of a car. It's good to have a set of skills."

To say the least …

Karen nodded absently, although it seemed her attention was lost again as she eyed him up and down. Dino pretended like he didn't notice her wandering stare as he reached for the axe and another block of wood.

"I should—"

"Stay and keep me company," Dino urged.

Karen's gaze snapped back up to Dino's face, but she didn't look as embarrassed this time to be caught staring. "I might bother you."

Dino laughed. "How?"

Karen shrugged. "A few different ways come to mind, and none of them involve helping you chop the wood."

The suggestive undertone to her words wasn't lost on Dino. "Stay."

She did.

Another ten minutes of Dino chopping wood and Karen not even trying to hide the fact she was staring passed them by. It was only when Dino tossed the axe back into the corner, done with the task, did Karen speak again.

She'd perched herself up on the edge of an old picnic table. Leaning back, she used her palms for support to keep her upright, while her beautiful legs hung over the side, swinging to and fro.

"I should have brought my camera out for this."

Dino's brows arched. "Why?"

"Your body—it would have made nice pictures."

Dino glanced down, picking out at least five scars right off the bat on his torso—imperfections, marks left from his years of abuse, amongst other things.

"I'm not sure about that," he finally said.

Karen snorted. "You're beautiful. Men never have to work very hard—women *think* about eating a piece of cake and gain five pounds from guilt."

"I work out all the time," Dino replied before he could think better of it. "It keeps me distracted and makes me too exhausted to think."

"Oh?"

"All the time. My brother is the same way, but he wouldn't admit it. We're not exactly … friends."

Karen glanced away, her brow furrowing. "You've never mentioned a brother."

"Theo. He was the guy that was vetting the dancers at the club on the night you showed up looking for a job."

Recognition dawned in Karen's eyes, and she turned red all over again. "Oh, my God. No wonder you haven't introduced me."

Dino shook his head, wanting to get her thoughts away from whatever crazy place it was currently in. "Trust me, that's not why."

"Then why not?"

"Nothing to tell," Dino said gruffly. "My brother and I, we're not like that, anyway."

It wasn't a total lie.

"I have a sister, too," Dino added. "Lily."

"Huh."

Karen still looked a bit dejected. Dino couldn't have that. This was supposed to be a good weekend for her, and he didn't want nonsense to ruin it for her. Strolling over to where she sat on the picnic table, Dino placed his hands under the skirt of Karen's summer dress, feeling the silky smoothness of her thighs against his palms.

"Smile," he murmured, inching forward until her lips were just a breath away from his. "It makes me happy to see you smile."

Karen did, and then leaned forward just enough to kiss him softly. The softness in the kiss didn't last for long—it never did between them.

She was like a drug.

He always wanted more.

Dino spread Karen's legs wider as he kissed her deeper, stepping closer and fitting himself tightly between her thighs. He tilted her head back, his tongue spearing into her mouth to war with hers. He loved the taste of her. Her softness and warmth never ended.

A low, pleased hum built in the back of Karen's throat. It echoed, reverberating straight through Dino's entire body, washing his bloodstream with lust, and shooting straight down to his cock. Under his dark wash jeans, his length hardened and grew, making him painfully aware of his now aching erection.

Karen's legs wrapped around his waist, her heels digging into his lower back and pulling him even closer to her body. The cotton between her thighs pressing to his straining cock under his jeans was nothing more than a tease. He needed more of her. Always.

"You know, I didn't come out here to fuck, Dino."

He wasn't really listening. He was more interested in pulling her dress higher while he kissed and nipped a path over the expanse of her neck. The taste of her was heavenly—addicting.

"Do you want me to stop?" he asked roughly.

Karen's legs tightened around him again. "Hell no."

Good enough.

"Shit ... here, let me ..."

Dino trailed off, more inclined to show Karen what he wanted rather than waste time explaining it. His arm circled her waist, and he pulled her into his embrace and off the old picnic table at the same time. Her surprised gasp and then light laughter filled the air; he never felt more satisfied than when he heard that sound come from her and he was the cause of it. Easily, as though she didn't weigh a thing, Dino turned them both around so *he* was the one sitting on the table, and she was in his lap.

"That's better," he said.

Karen smiled. "You *were* the one doing all the work out here."

"Exactly."

"My turn to do some work, Dino."

Dino didn't get the chance to question Karen on what she meant before she was pushing out of his lap, her feet dropping to the ground. He understood perfectly well what she meant when her fingers ghosted over the bulge of his erection before she worked to get his button undone and the zipper pulled down.

"Up," she ordered.

Dino obeyed, lifting his hips enough for her to tug his jeans down, his boxer-briefs following the same path. Her hands slipped under the black briefs and her warm palms found his hard cock, wrapping his length in a tight grip as she pulled his member free.

"Relax," he heard her whisper.

Dino had been distracted by the sight of Karen's fingers wrapping around his cock, the sensation of her fisting his length making him suddenly stupid in the head and damn near unable to speak. He hadn't realized he had actually just been holding his breath.

"I'm enjoying the show," he said.

Karen grinned sinfully. "It's about to get a lot better."

He didn't doubt that.

Karen's head dipped down low. Dino's hand instinctively fisted into the strands of her hair, and then all he could feel was the satin smooth warmth of her mouth on his cock. She didn't give him the chance to take another breath before she was taking him deeper into her throat, almost making him want to lay the hell back and let her go right to town.

Instead, Dino stayed upright, watching Karen below him, sucking him off. Her lips tightened wonderfully at his base, and on the up slide, the lightest scrape of her teeth drove him fucking wild. The glimmer of saliva wetting his length and the way her lips turned a little pinker the longer and harder she sucked him was a beautiful sight.

Fuck, yeah.

He *really* liked the show.

"Suck that cock, sweetheart."

Karen's approving hum built in her chest, vibrating the base of Dino's dick. He wanted to keep letting her do her thing—let her suck him fucking dry and swallow every drop he had to give her. He forced himself to drag her up from his cock, wanting to give her just as much as she gave him.

"I was having fun," she said, pouting.

Dino laughed huskily. "Yeah, me too. Too much; that's the problem. You need some fun, too."

He pulled Karen high to stand, kissing her hard as he slipped off the picnic table at the same time. Turning them around, Karen didn't hesitate to bend over the table when Dino urged her to turn and pressed his hand to her lower back. He pushed the skirt of her dress over her ass, his hand fitting perfectly against her backside.

Karen pushed back into his hand a second before his palm snapped along the swell of where her ass met the back of her thigh. Her skin turned the sweetest shade of pink instantly. Dragging his fingers down the line of her thong, he swept the digits under the material, only to find she was already wet, and so damned hot against his fingertips.

Dino swallowed hard as he stroked her with his fingers. "That gets you wet, huh?"

Karen looked back over her shoulder at him. "Hmm?"

"Sucking me off—it gets you wet."

She didn't look the least bit ashamed when she said, "Seems so."

Fuck.

Dino wasn't willing to wait any longer for what he wanted. He pulled Karen's thong down over her thighs and the stretchy material dropped to her ankles before she widened her stance a bit for him. His hand ran up her spine, feeling the tremor spreading over her skin, as he lined the head of his cock up with her glistening sex.

That first thrust was heaven.

The second was a tight bliss.

Dino wasn't one for soft and slow when he fucked, because it was usually nothing more than a need he was filling, but it wasn't quite the same with Karen. Even when he fucked her harder, he still felt a need to be soft in some way.

His fingers dancing over her skin.

A kiss to her shoulder blade.

Whispered words in her ear.

He needed those things for her just as much, if not more, than he needed to fill the need. It was strange and wonderful and terrifying, all at the same time.

"Oh, *God*," Karen mumbled.

She held tight to the table for purchase, her profile washed in bliss.

That was probably the best sight of all.

Dino didn't relent in his harsh, fast pace, not even when she came the first time … or the second time when his fingers had slipped between her thighs to find her clit and work it, too.

He held back from coming until she begged him to; until she was looking over her shoulder again, asking him for it, *wanting* it.

Then he came.

And only then.

CHAPTER 22

"WAVE to the detectives," Theo said as Dino stepped out of the club.

The club was closed given it was early morning, but that didn't mean it was shut down entirely. A lot of Dino's business on the illegal side of things happened throughout the day at the club, like *exchanges*. Dealers came in with money and left with product, for example.

"What?"

"Wave." Theo pointed and then waved, only his middle finger popped up at the same time. "See, wave at them. Right over there."

Sure enough, just across the parking lot, two men leaned against an unmarked, dark sedan. Dino wasn't sure if it was his lifestyle or history with cops and FBI agents, but he couldn't miss one even if he tried. Maybe it was the way they all dressed—slacks, dress shirts, and cheap blazers—or perhaps it was the way they carried themselves.

Or shit, maybe it was the stink that wafted off them.

The stench of *cop*.

Regardless of *what* it was that made officials so obvious to Dino, fact was, he didn't like to deal with them at all. It had been literally beaten into him that no matter what kind of cop they were, they all came out smelling the same when they were either dead, or had a man locked up.

"Showed up about ten minutes ago," Theo informed. "One of the guys came to let me know."

Dino adjusted his jacket, still watching the pair of detectives from the corner of his eye. "They didn't approach anyone?"

"Not yet." Theo shrugged, his cigarette bouncing on his lips as he spoke. "But then again, maybe they didn't need to approach someone because the person they were looking for hadn't showed themselves yet."

Dino understood perfectly well what Theo was saying.

Maybe the cops were waiting on *him*.

Why, Dino didn't know.

"You're clean, right?" Theo asked when Dino didn't immediately reply.

Dino bristled, feeling as though Theo had just thrown one hell of an accusation at him without a care in the world. An accusation that burned like acid.

"If you're asking if I have recently gained the same affliction our father had and turned informant for the police, I haven't."

"That's not—"

Dino stepped away from his brother, not willing to hear whatever it was Theo planned to say to him. "Later, man."

Theo cursed under his breath, but instead of saying something else, he wisely chose to head back inside the club. Of course, not without tossing another look over his shoulder at the men still casually leaning against the car.

Now, unfortunately, those men had turned their gazes on Dino.

He made every effort to avoid the police on a good day, but being involved with the Outfit meant he always had *someone* watching him—usually FBI. He was almost positive they had a damn board dedicated to just him, and everything they knew about him and his position within the Outfit. Any made man got that sort of attention from the officials, and even those who weren't made, but liked to make a fucking spectacle about their affiliation to the mob probably had their own special place in the cops' hearts, too. If nothing else, because cops had a habit of building cases over a period of time, and then using what they had as a threat of sorts against the man to frighten them with serious jail time, or ... turning rat.

Dino was not immune to that tactic simply because he had a Capo title.

Especially considering his uncle was the underboss of the operation, and Dino's own father had once been a rat for the officials, it all swirled around to leave him with a big, fat bullseye on his back. He wasn't sure if they thought he was the weak link in the chain that made up the Chicago mob, or what it was, but over the years, Dino had been approached more times than he cared to admit by police. They almost always approached him under the pretense that they just wanted to *talk*.

Nothing else.

Talk.

Dino wasn't up to talking with police, so like he had all the times before, he kept his head down and focused on getting the hell out of their presence as soon as he possibly could. Apparently, it wasn't going to work with these men, not that he thought it would.

"DeLuca, got a minute?" the shorter of the two detectives shouted at him.

Glancing up at the overcast sky, Dino blew out a heavy breath and silently told whoever was supposed to be looking out for him up above that they could take a flying fucking leap off the closest high wall.

"Not today," Dino said never once giving the men his attention. "Busy day; call my lawyer and he'll set up a time."

Dino was even kind enough to rattle off the number to his lawyer for the fools, hoping to God that they would take the hint and run with it.

Run far away from him.

"It's not the sort of thing you need a lawyer for, DeLuca," the other detective said.

The two detectives crossed the few parking spaces between their car and Dino's, putting less space between them until there was nothing left but a couple of feet. It instantly made Dino nervous, setting him on an edge that forced him to balance carefully between publicly acceptable behavior with police that *wouldn't* get him arrested, and privately acceptable behavior for the Outfit that *wouldn't* get him fucking killed.

It was the kind of edge no man in the Outfit wanted to be put on.

It was exactly why they all avoided cops like the plague.

It only took one single whisper from one person to another that someone else had been seen talking to cops like they were friendly and there the man would be—fucked.

He might as well have signed his own death warrant.

Dino did not want to be that man.

Shoving his hands in his pockets, Dino slightly turned his shoulder and back to the detectives, letting them know he wasn't open to talking while also making his body language clear for anyone else who might see that he didn't *want* or *invite* this attention. It was a game he had learned to play well, especially after seeing other men—men like his own father—be slaughtered for their mistakes with police.

"Are you deaf?" Dino asked, his gaze sweeping the parking lot as he spoke. "Or did you not understand when I said I've got a busy day?"

"We understand."

"Then take a hint and get lost."

"We're good. Agents Stanley and Courtly from—"

"Fuck," Dino uttered, pulling his keys out and hitting the unlock button on the fob.

Yeah, he'd messed up.

He'd assumed the two were just plain-clothed detectives come to rattle his chains like the many times before. He certainly hadn't thought the two were FBI as those fucking idiots rarely bothered him unless something big was about to go down.

Dino had just grabbed the handle of the driver's door when the agent stopped him by saying, "How many businesses do you own in Chicago, DeLuca?"

Christ.

"A few," Dino answered.

"Do you use all of them for Outfit business, or just the club?"

Dino didn't know what the agents were getting at, but he didn't like it. His teeth grinded in his effort to stay quiet, but he still spoke even though he knew he shouldn't. "What does the FBI have anything to do with *my* business? Chicago PD getting lazy and they called you in? I'm pretty sure my business is below the level of the Bureau."

"War on crime?" the taller of the two—Courtly—asked.

Dino scoffed. "Right—the *war*. Like the war on drugs that actually only created *more* drugs. Or the war on guns, which only left Chicago with *more* bodies piling up. If that's your mode of operation, you people are fucking failing. Miserably. Try again."

Agent Stanley stepped forward, a strange smile curling his lips.

"Keen observation skills you have there, Dino. I bet it does you well as a Capo, huh?"

"I'm not even going to respond to that."

The man shrugged. "Didn't think you would."

Agent Courtly glanced around the parking lot. "Three-hundred-million this year was dedicated to fighting the war on crime, but of course, we all know that starts at *home*, right? How much Outfit business is tied to overseas trading and exporting? How much business is tied to *importing*? We're just doing our jobs, DeLuca."

"And I'm done wasting time on this today," Dino replied, opening his car door.

He had just slid inside his vehicle when Agent Stanley grabbed the edge of the door, keeping Dino from closing it completely. The agent didn't even grace Dino with his attention when he demanded he let go, given he wasn't under any sort of arrest and they had no reason to be bothering him.

"Thought we'd give you a heads-up," the agent said quietly. "Maybe give you a chance to do something worthy with your life."

"What are you *talking* about?" Dino barked.

The agent looked Dino right in the face, and smiled. "Seems someone is out to make a mess for you."

What?

That question seemed to be the story of Dino's life lately.

Instead of asking the agent to explain himself again—he knew damn well he wouldn't get a decent answer—Dino pulled hard on his door, forcing the man to let go or get all of his fingers broken when it slammed shut. Thankfully, the fool let go, leaving both agents standing outside of his car as Dino started the engine, backed out of the parking space, and pulled away with tires squealing against the pavement.

But even as he drove away, his mind was frozen.

He was stuck on the whole encounter, as strange and random as it had seemed. He was one person who knew all too well that no matter how odd something seemed, coincidences did not exist in their life.

Dino could still hear the agent's words all too loudly in the back of his mind.

Someone is out to make a mess for you.

What did that mean?

What in the fuck does that even mean?

Dino decided he would have to figure that out later, because at that moment, he had far more important things to consider. Like the fact the agents had specifically thought to mention his club, and the business that he conducted inside.

That was more important.

That was something he could handle immediately.

Hitting the call button on the steering wheel, the car's Bluetooth turned on, chiming loudly with instructions.

"Call Theo," Dino said.

Seconds later, the call rang through. It took three rings for Theo to pick up, and for that, Dino was grateful. Sometimes when his brother was in a mood, he wouldn't pick up a call from Dino at all. He certainly hadn't left his brother with the best attitude at the club.

"What?" Theo demanded when the call connected.

"We've got—maybe, I don't know—a problem."

Theo sighed harshly, the sound crackling over the speakers. "Speak in a language the rest of us understand, Dino. I don't have time for bullshit today."

Fine.

If that was the way Theo wanted to do things.

Dino could do that.

"Clear out the club," he demanded. "Everything related to the crew—the books, dope, whatever—get it out."

Theo balked. "All of it? It'll take weeks to get the whole crew up to speed on new details and—"

"Do what I said. Get it out before tomorrow morning. Make damn sure nothing is left, and wherever you move it all to, it's not connected to another one of my businesses."

Dino wasn't taking risks.

He didn't know what was going on exactly, or what *might* happen.

But something might.

That was all that mattered. Something *might* happen, someone was watching, and he was not going to get caught up in the mess that was left behind when it did go down.

"The detectives?" Theo asked, clearly choosing his words carefully.

"Not detectives—*agents*."

Theo cursed heavily.

Dino understood the feeling.

"All right, I'll get it cleaned up," Theo finally said. "What about your other businesses—you hide money in those books, Dino. It's not as easy to clean that up, you know?"

"Don't worry about it."

The club would have to do, Dino knew.

The rest ... the rest would have to wait.

Or he would have to deal with it.

"What are you doing right now?" Theo asked.

Dino stared out at the road ahead of him, barely blinking an eye as he sped up a bit more and passed another line of slow moving vehicles. He knew exactly where he was heading because it seemed to be the only place he ever wanted to go when shit was not going as planned and he needed a break.

Karen.

Of course, he wouldn't tell Theo that.

"Business in Wicker," Dino settled on saying. "I'll be at the club in the morning as usual. Make sure what I asked for has been done by then."

That was all Dino would offer.

Karen was still untouched by the Outfit.

He intended to keep her that way.

CHAPTER 23

THE most beautiful sight, Dino decided, was Karen sleeping with navy blue sheets tangled around her body in a disarray as though she'd been tossing and turning. Her naked legs peeked out through the sheets, and the swell of her hip drew his gaze upward to where her hand rested on his side of the bed.

His side.

It was a strange thought, and certainly not something he was used to thinking. Or even *having*, for that matter.

Dino knew it was true. Despite how strange their relationship was, and how he often came and went without any real explanation, it was *true*. Karen never complained, and she often smiled at him come morning when she found him tucked into her bed with his arm slung around her waist, keeping her tight to his body.

She never asked for more.

That was probably what Dino loved the most about her.

It was also what scared him the most.

Would she wake up one day and want more?

He didn't know if he could give it to her.

Silently, Dino shed his clothes and slipped into the bed, his arms finding Karen's waist as he dragged her closer to him and then buried his face in the crook of her neck.

She smelled like heaven and home.

With her, he didn't dream horrible things, or at least not as often.

With her, he was calm and content.

With her, there was peace.

The very second he was in her bed, surrounded by soft sheets where he could soak in her warmth and pretend like the outside world didn't exist, everything was perfectly *fine*. The thoughts that had constantly plagued him on the drive over disappeared, melting from his mind without a second of hesitation.

His worries were gone as he pulled her body closer into his, thoroughly enjoying how well her curves fit into his hard lines. It was her day off from the restaurant, and in usual Karen fashion, he wasn't surprised to find her sleeping in. Dino didn't want to wake her from the dreams she was so clearly enjoying—if the lax expression of happiness on her features was any indication—so he was extra careful not to wake her.

It took every bit of willpower he had inside not to get her up just so he could pull those sheets away and explore.

Dino knew she wouldn't complain—hell, she'd probably be happy he had woke her up—but he liked to watch her sleep, too.

This was good.

"Hey," he heard whispered.

Her raspy voice made him smile. Apparently, he hadn't needed to wake her up; she did that all on her own.

"Didn't mean to wake you," he said, kissing her bare shoulder.

Karen stretched in his arms like a little kitten waking up from a long nap. "This is good, Dino."

Like always, he could only stand to have Karen naked and in his hands for so long before he was acting on the thrumming lust washing through his veins. Her breathless laugh echoed in the apartment when Dino rolled them over, putting her on top of him. All her caramel waves tumbled over her shoulders, and he sifted his fingers through the strands, enjoying the silkiness.

It wasn't long before she was lifting her hips, her hand snaking between her thighs to grab the base of his cock, and then she was lowering down.

Painfully slow …

Tight, wet heat engulfed his length and for one suspended moment, the world was right and lovely again.

With Karen, it was always lovely.

"Jesus," Dino grunted out as she settled on top of him fully.

Karen's lips curved into a sensual, pleased smile. The sleepiness hadn't fully left, so that dazed look in her eyes made her seem almost high. Her teeth cut into her bottom lip as her hips shifted, and every silken inch of her pussy clenched around his cock, holding him tight and taking away his breath for that split second.

"This is how you wake up," Karen whispered.

Dino had to agree, even if he wasn't the one being woken up. Whatever she wanted in that moment, he was inclined to agree with her, as long as she kept circling her hips like she was. It was driving him fucking *crazy*.

In a good way.

"Karen," Dino said.

"Mmm."

Her lashes fluttered over her cheeks as her eyes closed, her body lifting and lowering down on him slower than before. Each time she came down, he felt that telltale tremor crawl over her skin, and she seemed to heat right up under his hands.

"Hey," he said, the word catching slightly in his throat.

Karen swallowed audibly, her tongue peeking out to wet her lips, but she never once opened her eyes. "Yeah?"

Dino's hand traveled up the flat expanse of her stomach, between the valley of her breasts, and stopped at the column of her throat. The delicate line of her shoulders shuddered as his fingers wrapped around her throat, and her pulse drummed hard under his hold. Never too tight, he knew, but just enough to let her know he was there, that he could *feel* her life beating under his fingertips.

Then, her body lowered on his a little faster—harder.

His free hand found the dip in her waist, his fingers digging in hard enough to leave the imprint of his touch behind, but she didn't seem to mind the roughness.

In fact, she sighed.

And smiled again.

Dino let out a shaky breath, willing the pressure building in his spine to leave, if only for a moment. Fucking Karen was a dream—one he never wanted to wake up from. Still, he wasn't quite ready for the dream to end, and if she continued what she was doing, it was going to come to a stop a hell of a lot faster than both of them wanted.

Of that, Dino was most sure.

"Look at me."

His demand came out harsher than he intended it to, but that was only because he was so focused on the way Karen looked on top of him with her head tossed back as she rode him, that he couldn't tamper the desperation coloring his words.

Karen didn't seem to mind as her eyes flew wide open instantly, seeking him out as her hands came to lay flat on the railroad path of his abdominal muscles. If anything, that bit of leverage gave her the ability to ride his cock faster than before.

"You're going to make me come," Dino warned.

Her teasing smile said that was *exactly* what she wanted to happen.

He wasn't ready to yet.

"Have I told you," Karen said, a breathless quality curling around the edges of her words, "that you're the most beautiful when you're fucking me?"

Dino's hands squeezed her a little harder. "Beautiful is the word you want to use?"

"Real. Raw. *Ridiculously beautiful.* Pick one."

He didn't need to.

It was how she seen him, not the other way around.

It wasn't for him to decide.

"You've never told me," he said.

Karen's tongue wet her lips again, a soft trembling moan following the action. "Sometimes I think when I feel so strongly about something—some*one*—that it must be clear enough that I don't have to *say* it, too."

She watched him under her lowered lashes, never once stopping the rhythm of her body moving on top of his. Every lower of her hips was accompanied by the slap of skin against skin, and the clench of her inner muscles around his length.

It was almost teasing.

"Karen," Dino started to say, wanting to stop her from saying something she couldn't take back.

Or worse, that he might have to take away.

Because while he was entirely distracted by her—by fucking her—he still *heard* her. He heard what she was saying, or rather, what she was trying to say to him. He understood those feelings she didn't vocalize, because he felt them beating through his bloodstream every single time he was in her presence.

That didn't mean he had to say it.

Right?

Shouldn't she just know?

He *knew*.

"I forget that just because I feel something, it doesn't mean you know I feel it," Karen continued.

He was worried he was going to break her heart someday.

He was frightened that because he couldn't give her something healthy—something normal—that they would never be good enough for one another.

He was scared she wouldn't understand.

Still, Dino was all too aware that with this—like with the way she saw him—it wasn't something he was allowed to have a say in. It seemed he had already had his say in her feelings where they were concerned, and his fears simply didn't factor into it at all.

Karen was allowed to *feel*.

She was not like him.

She didn't have to hide from it.

So he let her say it; he let her whisper the words in his ear after he'd twisted them around and put her on her knees. He'd let her tell him exactly how she felt because she had every right to say it after he'd pounded into her from behind and made her beg for more.

"I love you," she'd told him.

Three little words.

Spoken quietly.

Quickly said, mumbled into a pillow.

He loved her, too.

It just wasn't that simple.

"Coffee?" Dino called out to Karen.

"Tea—it's in the same spot."

He thought that was a little odd, considering Karen rarely, if ever, drank tea, but he didn't question her on it, simply grabbed the box of decaffeinated tea and dropped a bag into the steaming mug.

"Want me to bring it in there, or are you going to peel your ass out of bed?" Dino asked.

Karen laughed lightly from the bedroom. "I'm comfortable, Dino. It's my day off and I've had a crappy week. Stop judging me. Milk and one sugar."

"No judging. I'll bring it."

He *almost* asked why her week had been crappy, but decided against it, if only because he was about to add to her stress when he was going to have to warn her about the agents, and the possibility that they may be around asking questions. It was a simple enough task as far as demanding his employees of all his businesses deflect any attention from officials, but Karen wasn't *just* Dino's employee.

Once the tea was steeped long enough, he grabbed his coffee and Karen's mug and made his way back into the bedroom. Karen, resting against the headboard with a book in her hands, looked like she had spent the night rolling in the sheets with him.

She looked properly fucked with her lazy smile and messy hair, not to mention the sheets she had pulled up around her body to keep her modesty.

Not that it did anything to hide her body.

He knew all too well what she looked like under that sheet.

"Here," he said, handing her tea over.

Karen took it with a happy sigh, sipping on the hot liquid. "It's good."

"Tea is new for you."

She didn't look at him when she replied, "Didn't think you'd notice the change."

Dino's brow furrowed. "Why wouldn't I notice something like that?"

"It's not important. Come here."

He did as she asked, leaning over the bed and letting her pull him close enough for a kiss. Her lips curved into a smile against his mouth as she stroked his cheek with her thumb.

"I do, you know," she said softly, "love you."

Dino wished it was as easy for him to say as it was for her. She could let the words fall from her mouth so easily, as if it was the same thing as breathing.

For him, a fear choked him silent when he wanted to reply in kind—reply honestly. She was entirely his, had never said a thing differently, but Dino knew the things that were his, things that he loved, could be taken away without reason or apology.

Still, he managed to say the words.

She deserved to hear them.

"Love you, sweetheart," Dino murmured.

Karen's smile bloomed into a full blown grin. "The tea *is* new."

"Decaffeinated, too. What good does that do?"

"Suffices my need for a hot drink."

"Why the change?" Dino asked.

Karen didn't answer right away, instead dropping her gaze and her hand from his face. Dino leaned back, standing straight as he watched her curiously.

What was she hiding?

"What brought you over here this early?" Karen asked.

A deflection.

Dino was not a stupid man.

He saw that for exactly what it was.

"I'll indulge you for a minute, but then you're going to tell me what you're hiding," Dino said frankly.

Karen still wouldn't look at him, but she nodded. "Fair enough."

"I wanted to see you; I haven't been able to have a minute with you since we got back from the cabin two weeks ago. Something else came up today and it made sense for me to come over while I had the chance."

"Something else came up?"

Dino took a deep breath—*now or never.* He wanted to keep Karen blind and deaf to his business as much as possible, but sometimes, he knew he wasn't going to have a choice, especially if she might somehow be dragged into it by affiliation. This was one of those times.

"Police might be sniffing around," he said, choosing what he told her carefully.

'Agents' would have been honest, but it would have needed a better explanation. He chose to go with telling her it was police simply to make the situation seem less *bad.*

"Oh?" Karen asked, glancing up at him with genuine concern in her eyes.

"Don't worry about it—it's nothing. But if someone does come around asking questions, follow everyone else's lead and say you know nothing."

"I can do that."

Dino smiled, thankful. "Good. Now what are you hiding?"

Karen's hands tightened around the mug, and she dropped his stare again. "I …"

He didn't like that she seemed scared to speak—scared of him, maybe.

That cut him to the core.

"Whatever it is, just tell me," Dino urged.

Short of her saying she had given information to the officials, Dino could handle it.

Surely.

Karen finally looked back at him the fear still coloring her eyes with a vibrancy. Yet when she spoke, she did so with strength, as though she was ready for *anything*. "I'm pregnant, Dino. Eleven weeks, almost three months. I've been busy and overlooked the fact I'd missed a couple cycles. We're not always safe—this morning, for example, not that we needed to be, but *you* didn't know. I found out shortly after we got back from the cabin."

He could handle it.

That's what he had said.

That's what he had thought.

Pregnant.

Except that, he knew.

Dino wasn't sure he could handle that.

He should be excited. He was not a young man—he was capable of caring and providing for a child of his. He loved Karen, and she was right, he could have taken precautions to prevent this very thing from happening.

It should not have been a surprise.

It still *was*.

He was not ready for this.

Fear kept him silent, and instinctively, to protect Karen from unknowns that would love to hurt her and his unborn child simply because they were *his*, Dino took a step away, moving back from her.

Karen's features fell, hurt coloring her eyes. "Dino."

He took another step back even knowing he was hurting her because he didn't know what else to do to *protect* her. The only way he could do that was by removing himself from the equation.

171

Anything that was not given to him was always taken away.

That fear was so *real* to him.

So alive.

He wouldn't let her be hurt because she was his.

He would rather hurt her himself than see her be used against him.

Karen wouldn't understand.

Dino wouldn't explain it.

CHAPTER 24

"IF you're not up to discussing business today, that's fine. But don't ignore me as though you've got better fucking things to be doing," Riley Conti said. "I'll take your lack of conversation as your usual bullshit, but the rest is just disrespectful, Dino."

The bitter tone of the Outfit's front boss held an almost threatening quality to it, and that was the only thing that made Dino glance up from his clenched hands.

Riley glared at him from across the restaurant table. His outburst, and Dino's lack of attention, had not gone unnoticed by the other men who had been brought to attend the meeting between the front boss and Capo.

"Well, do you?" Riley barked.

Dino willed away the mess in his mind, determined to get this day over with so he could move on. "Do I, what?"

"Have better things to be doing, Dino!"

Yes, he wanted to say.

He should be with Karen, across the fucking city, apologizing for being a total asshole the week before. He should be on his knees in front of her, making amends in whatever way she wanted him to for leaving her place without so much as a goodbye. He should be feeding his desires, placating the dull pain in his heart by going to *her*.

Instead, he was sitting in a shitty restaurant having a conversation with a man he cared nothing for. Dino felt more for shit under his shoe than he did for Riley Conti.

Business was still business.

He had a job to do.

"I'm here, aren't I?" Dino asked calmly. "You want more foot traffic on your territory, fine. I'll make it happen."

"With *my* men—not your brother doing the majority of the work."

Dino resisted the urge to roll his eyes. "Still don't like Theo, huh?"

Riley didn't grace that with a response.

Honestly, he didn't need to.

"Do I need to take this to Ben?" Riley asked after a moment of silence had stretched on between the men.

At that, Dino did tense in his seat. He'd gone through much of the meeting without trouble, despite his lack of conversation and attention. It really wasn't that unusual for him, regardless of what Riley wanted to say.

But at that statement—that threat—Dino did hesitate.

Riley *knew* it was a good threat to use. The front boss was one of few men aware of just how to get what he wanted where Dino was concerned, and that was through Ben.

"I said you'd get the foot traffic," Dino said.

"Make it happen, or the next chat I have will be with your uncle."

With that final threat hanging over Dino, the front boss stood from his seat, waved a hand at his son across the restaurant and the other men who had attended the meeting, and then he was gone. Dino only looked up from his hands again when he heard the jingle of the bell above the restaurant's front door.

Being alone did nothing to settle the anxiety drumming in his heart. He was not on his game, and this meeting proved it even more. He was sleeping less and less, and when he did sleep, it was as though he'd dipped his mind into hell for a few hours.

Dino knew what his problem was—he was without Karen.

It was a jackass move to leave her without explanation after she'd told him about the pregnancy, but he didn't know what else to do. He wanted to protect her from the monsters in his life—including himself—but the only way to do that was to cut her off completely.

Pregnant, his mind taunted. *While she's pregnant with your child.*

Dino never pretended to be a good guy, or even an honorable one, for that matter. Even this was kind of low for him, and he knew it all too well.

"Fucking hate that tool," Theo muttered from beside Dino as he took a seat at the table.

He'd forgotten that his brother was there—yet another reminder he was way off his game and that meant he was probably about to suffer for it.

"I'll handle Riley," Dino said.

He tried to sound flippant, but was sure he failed in the effort. Theo didn't mention it either way, and for that Dino was grateful.

"And what was that shit he tried to pull at the end about Ben?" Theo asked.

Dino pushed up from his chair, trying to appear unaffected. "You know what it was."

Theo glanced away. "Yeah, I guess I do."

That was that.

"Do us all a favor and put some guys in Riley's streets to do whatever work he wants them doing," Dino said. "It'll keep him happy and off our backs for a while. I've got enough going on without that asshole adding to it."

"Got it."

It took from the time Dino left the restaurant to the second he sat down in the driver's seat of his car to decide to call Karen. He'd done well all week by avoiding her, but the fact remained the same, he didn't *want* to avoid her at all.

Knowing she *should* be at work, he called through to the restaurant first. The office phone rang off the hook with no one picking up the call. Confused, Dino hung up, then tried another number—Karen's cell.

That too rang with no answer.

A heavy feeling settled in Dino's gut as he made an illegal U-turn right in the middle of the street, uncaring if he got pulled over and ticketed for the action. Something wasn't right—he could feel it in his *bones*.

Karen was habitual to a fault. She didn't miss work, she didn't ignore calls, and even if she was pissed off to the high heavens at him, she wouldn't snub a call from him.

Surely not *now*.

Knowing Karen should be working, he headed to the restaurant first. Surprisingly, Dino found Karen's car was not parked in the lot with the rest of the employees', and when he went inside, he didn't find her there, either. He by-passed other employees, disregarding their questioning stares as he flew through the main dining area and then the kitchen, heading straight for the back offices.

Her car wasn't there, so she shouldn't be either.

That didn't stop Dino from checking the office.

It was empty.

Not entirely empty, as things were still in its place, but Karen was not inside working as she should be. Even her laptop was gone.

Dino had just turned around to leave when the buzzing of his phone in his pocket stopped him. He checked the caller ID, seeing Karen's name light up the screen, and quickly slammed the office door shut, determined not to have his conversation overheard.

"Where are you?" Dino asked the second he picked up the call.

Maybe that was not the best way he could have answered, given everything. Dino was well aware that he had no right to be playing the asshole between the two of them. He was the one who walked out on her and then didn't even bother to give her a call for a week.

"Hello to you, too," Karen muttered.

"I'm at the restaurant and you're not here. You're on the schedule, Karen."

He sounded like an asshole.

Dino tried to check that impulse and put it in place, but he wasn't sure it was going to do any good. Especially not after what she said next.

"I quit, so no, I don't need to be there at all."

"You *quit*."

It didn't even come out as a question.

Karen sighed. "Yeah—I'm done."

"Karen …" Dino took a breath, thinking hard on what he wanted to say next because he knew it was going to be important. It was going to mean the difference between her never wanting to see him again, and him being able to explain himself in a way that she might understand. "Give me ten minutes, please."

"For what, Dino?" she asked softly. "For you to walk out on me again? For you to leave me trying to figure out a shitty situation by myself *again*? I would rather do this alone than be with someone who makes me feel like I'm doing it alone. Do you understand what I'm saying?"

Yes.

He absolutely did.

"I don't want you to do it alone," Dino said. "I'm sorry that I was a fucking asshole last week. I could say you took me by surprise and I didn't know how to react, so what you got was just a really bad reaction, but it would only be half of the truth."

"Listen—"

"No, let me finish. I've had the shittiest week in a long time, although I am sure yours has been worse than mine. I don't know what to do, but if you just let me explain it, maybe you'd understand *why*."

Dino had fully intended to keep Karen out of his business as far as the Outfit and his family went. He didn't want to put her in a position where Ben might be able to use her to hurt Dino in some way, or God forbid, as another one of his *lessons*.

But if it would make her understand *why* he kept her at a distance, if explaining to her how his fears were like a constant noose tightening around his neck every single day of his life, then he would do it.

He didn't know what would come after.

He wasn't sure that those details mattered at the moment.

"Ten minutes," Dino said almost pleadingly. "Please give me ten minutes with you to explain. I love you—that should be enough for ten minutes."

He'd said the words so easily that time.

Easy, he knew, because he meant them and he didn't say things he didn't mean.

Karen hesitated on the other end of the call. "Fine. But that's all you get. Come over to my place now, and I'll give you ten minutes."

Dino was more than willing to agree to that, and with a quick goodbye, he was already heading out of his office.

He prided himself on the fact that he was not a stupid man. Truth be told, Karen was not a stupid woman, either. She was more than capable of handling herself, and taking care of her own business.

She didn't *need* him.

She had taken care of herself long before he'd ever come

along. She never accepted help from him beyond the job he gave her. He offered to help pay for bills when she came up short from time to time because he had more money than he knew what to do with, but Karen refused because she didn't need him to do anything.

Dino took comfort in the fact that his lover was able to keep her head above water and her feet on the ground, but he also knew what that really meant.

If she wanted to walk away from him, if she had finally had enough, she could do so.

She was not dependent on him.

Dino was only starting to realize now that it was him who was dependent on her in more ways than he cared to count. She made him happy, gave him peace. She made him smile, gave him happiness. She was light in the darkness that constantly clouded his life, and he had come to rely on her to keep shining around him when everything else seemed so dull.

In all his efforts to keep Karen from being pulled into his life, she had become the most important part of it.

Somehow, he had done that.

He just didn't know how to keep her light from being snuffed out because of it.

Dino figured he could handle all of that at another time. He would handle his uncle's disapproval over his relationship with an outsider, and what Ben might do because of it, at another time.

Right then, Karen was more important.

Dino owned her an apology *and* an explanation.

The ringing of a phone call echoing through the car's speakers brought Dino from his thoughts with a bang. He didn't think to check the caller ID, assuming it was probably Karen calling back to make sure he was still on his way to her place.

Theo's voice answering back when Dino picked up surprised him. "We've got a problem."

Dino groaned, his hands tightening hard around the steering wheel. "Not today, man. I've got other things to—"

"Doesn't matter," Theo interjected. "The club got raided, Dino."

Dino turned into a block of ice as he hit the breaks, damn near causing the car behind him to ram into his backend. He flipped the guy the middle finger as the man maneuvered his vehicle around Dino's to drive off.

"What did you just say?" Dino demanded.

"The club is being raided."

"Right now."

"Yeah," Theo confirmed.

"Police or—"

"FBI."

Fuck.

Dino's frustrations boiled over as he slammed his fists into the steering wheel.

"Sounded like they're working on other warrants," Theo continued, "for other places."

"Where?"

"Your guess is as good as mine, but it seemed like if they found what they were looking for at the club, the warrants would be approved on the spot."

Probably his place, Dino thought. Maybe his other businesses.

Dino checked the clock on his dashboard and noted the time. He could be home in five minutes from his current position. He had time to get there and destroy the papers and files in his safe that would basically put him away for years on fraud, tax evasion, money laundering and *more*.

Nobody ever said the mafia was clean living.

Dino knew that all too well.

He made another illegal U-turn.

Karen would have to wait—she would understand.

This time, he would finally explain.

CHAPTER 25

DINO didn't even bother to park his car properly once he was in the lot for his building. No, he just threw it in park right at the front door while leaving it running, ignored the man who tried to hold open the door for him, and bolted for the stairway.

He took four flights of stairs three steps at a time, a paralyzing fear working its way through his nervous system with each and every step. He didn't have the slightest clue whether or not the agents had gotten their warrants, if they were done at the club, on their way over to his place, or goddammit, how much time he even had.

If he had any time at all …

It seemed as though it took him entirely too long to get inside his place, but once he was, Dino wasted no time heading to his office. Ripping the painting from the wall, he tossed it to the floor, uncaring that the four-thousand dollar artwork hit the corner of the edge and tore. Behind the painting rested something far more precious—something *far* more valuable.

Dino spun the dial on the safe, hitting the numbers that would open it. His mother's birthdate, his father's death date, and then his siblings' birthdates. Pulling on the latch, the safe popped open, and the sweetest relief filled Dino at the sight of what rested within.

Papers. Documents.

Information.

There were other documents he knew he *should* worry about as well that was currently hidden within mountains of files in his filing cabinets. But frankly, the information was exactly that—a goddamn mountain to go through. Seeds of information planted within financial documents that would only lead to tidbits of data that may lead to something else. It would all take a while to get through, and even *if* someone managed to figure out where it all lead, it might only hurt him with a few fines and a bit of jail time.

No, he didn't give a single shit about what was in his filing cabinets.

It was the documentation in his safe that needed to go.

Dino pulled out papers and files in the handfuls, tossing them into a metal garbage can in one giant heap of *trouble*.

Trouble that could put him away for years upon years.

Offshore account information. Racket details and contracts. Falsified legal paperwork. Cooked books for a dozen businesses. Fraudulent tax filings. The list went on and on.

Some of the paperwork he would have to destroy would never be fully replaced, and in the end, that would mean lost money. Dino was all too aware of that knowledge, but that didn't stop him from grabbing the last few documents and the one file left inside the safe. Without even a moment of hesitation, he tossed it into the garbage can as well.

All that was left in his safe were stacks of bills that probably added up to a hundred thousand dollars all together.

Dino knew what might have been found at his club, and that left his brain racing a million miles a minute. Theo had done well to clean out the dirty business that would get Dino time in jail on drug charges—but the financial side of things, information that would prove the club was funneling money from all sorts of illegal activity, was still there, in the offices and hidden within the mountains of paperwork in the filing cabinets.

Dino was *fucked*.

One way or another, a jail cell was likely.

At least for a while.

So as he grabbed a lighter from his office desk and lit the corner of one of the papers in the garbage can on fire, he was already thinking about Karen.

Karen and his *child*.

What would she do now?

Who would she depend on?

He didn't think for a moment that she would understand, though he had thought before that she might if *he* were the one to explain it all to her.

Dino knew now that wouldn't be the case.

It would be one thing for Karen to know Dino was involved in illegal activities on a daily basis—she had a good idea about all of that nonsense, anyway. It would be an entirely other matter when she learned his whole life was built upon schemes, lies, and dirty money.

Schemes that left businesses bankrupt and hundreds out of jobs. Lies that left bodies in rivers with their hands and feet cut off where the scavengers could pick the corpses apart. Dirty money that paid for his lifestyle.

She wouldn't be able to understand any of that—who would?

Don't mess with outsiders, and especially not women, Ben would always tell the DeLuca brothers as they grew up, *they only bring more problems than they're worth.*

Dino had followed that rule up until he met Karen, and even after to an extent, by keeping her out of his business as much as he possibly could. He'd done it for both his own selfish reasons, and also to protect her from people like Ben.

A man who would kill her simply because Dino had gotten close to her, and because she was not brought up inside their smothering ways.

It certainly didn't help that Karen had also put her hands in Dino's books for one of his businesses. She'd falsified numbers for him when he added extra cash to the books in one of his many ways to hide dirty cash in a simple way. He didn't want her taking the hit for his shit; she wouldn't because he would do whatever he needed to make sure none of this fell back on her.

But he also needed to take care of her.

Her *and* his child.

Somehow.

He just didn't know where to start or how to go about doing anything in his current situation. As the small fire in the garbage can began to grow, a thick black plume of smoke and ash rising from the burning papers, Dino turned away from the sight and lifted his shirt to cover his mouth.

God knew he didn't need to be breathing his sins in as he was trying to destroy them. All too soon, those very sins would be biting him in the ass, and very possibly, locking him away for a good few years or more.

But as he turned away from the burning papers, the money in the safe caught his eye once more.

All over again, Dino was faced with a choice.

He could spend whatever little time he had left going through and destroying what papers and documents might be in his filing cabinets, or he could spent it giving Karen a *chance* to start over in some small way.

It wouldn't be a lot, but knowing her, she'd make it work.

Even if she hated him for it.

Even if she didn't touch it for months.

It was something and it could work.

Dino flung open another drawer in his desk, digging through plastic-sealed envelopes to find one that was big enough to hold the stacks of money he had inside his safe. Soon enough, he found a yellow one that just might do the trick.

The buzzing in his pocket started up again—another phone call.

Dino opted to ignore it, knowing good and damn well that it might be a call he needed to take. It could be Theo letting him know the officials were on their way, or something else. It might even be Karen wondering where in the hell he was, as he should have been at her place a good fifteen minutes ago.

If it were her, there was no doubt in his mind that this would be her final straw.

It was one thing for him to up and leave the week before.

It would be another for him to flake on her *again*.

While the whole situation was a giant misunderstanding that he was sure he could fix with a long, honest explanation, Dino wasn't sure if Karen would even be willing to hear it. Especially not if he was locked up—he couldn't have her around then anyway.

It would be a way for Ben to find her.

The thought made him sicker and colder than ever.

So instead of picking up the call, Dino went to work on the money in the safe. He grabbed handfuls of the cash, stuffing it into the large, bubble mailer as fast as he could while making sure there was enough room to fit most of it inside. Once he had filled the mailer with as much money as he could, Dino tossed it aside on the desk, reaching for one thing he always kept close at hand.

His black book—filled with contacts—flipped open to the desk. Dino started tearing out pages as he went, tossing them into the burning garbage can. While the great majority of the contacts were just normal, law abiding citizens, some belonged to people who couldn't afford to be tied up in a mess with a gangster who had gotten caught.

Finally, he got to the page he needed.

Karen's address and info stared back at him.

It was only her initials written on the page.

K.M.

It was yet *another* way that Dino had made an effort to keep her presence in his life quiet. Even if her details in his black book could simply be explained away by saying she was an employee of his. It hadn't mattered to him. He wanted to keep her as safe as he possibly could from his life.

Fuck.

How hard he was failing, he realized sadly.

Dino couldn't think on that realization for long, instead he went about writing Karen's address on the bubble mailer with a black marker, making sure her details were clear, bold, and couldn't be somehow screwed up when it went into the mail. On the return address section, he hesitated.

But only for a second.

In big, bold letters, Dino wrote, *DO NOT RETURN TO SENDER.*

He didn't want the money coming back to him. He didn't need it, Karen *would.* He hoped the one sentence would be enough for her to get his hint, take the money, and do what she needed with it, but he didn't know if it would be.

The woman was fucking stubborn.

He loved her for it, sure, but she could be difficult.

This was something he nor she could be difficult about. Karen would need a backup plan, even if she wouldn't fully understand why, and Dino needed to make sure she and his unborn child would be taken care of.

Deep in his heart, burrowing into his black soul, that need was taking hold.

It was far greater than even his need to make sure he was okay, that he came out unscathed in all of this.

She came first now.

His child would come first.

He had to make sure of that.

Ripping out a piece of paper from a notepad, Dino scribbled a few sentences, not taking much time to think about what he could or should say to Karen, but rather, the first things that came to his mind. Things that were important—things that would keep her safe.

Things that he needed her to know.

I'm sorry. Please use this, even if you don't want to. Know that I love you. Stay away.

Then, he hesitated on the last sentence he knew he absolutely needed to write—something he had to tell Karen, but knew how it would come across without an explanation to follow it, or for that matter, without him telling her why he was asking it of her.

Don't give the child my names.—Dino.

His hand had slipped on that final sentence, the trembling making his letters appear more haphazard than his writing usually was. His heart beat painfully hard in his chest as he took in the words again and again, rereading them to himself until his eyes hurt and his vision blurred. He hadn't realized how absolutely aching it would be to write those words, to know he had to mean them, and to know what it would mean and feel like to Karen when she was the one reading them.

Keep them safe, he kept telling himself.

It was starting to feel like a mantra.

He almost grabbed another paper and rewrote his short letter, wanting to take that last sentence out, wanting to tie himself and his legacy to a child not yet born. But he couldn't.

So he didn't.

Dino didn't let himself stare at the letter for too long lest he go back and change what he knew was best for Karen, instead he folded the paper into a small square and shoved it into the bubble mailer, too. Quickly but carefully, he sealed the package, grabbed the stack of prepaid mailing stickers, and stuck as many onto the package as he could. It was probably too many, but at least then it wouldn't get lost to the system for having too little.

It was only then that Dino realized his entire office was filled with a hazy cloud of smoke, lingering midway in the room like a heavy blanket waiting to fall. For a long moment, he stared at the haze, hoping he had done enough to at least save himself a life sentence.

A year, he could handle.

A few years would put him back a lot, but it was still manageable.

A life sentence was a death warrant.

Dino didn't know how much time he had left, if any at all, so he didn't bother to start going through his filing cabinets to destroy what was in them, too. Instead, he headed back out of his apartment, making his way down to the end of the hall where he knew he could finish at least one thing that was far more important than the rest—without problem or the officials finding out he had done so.

The evidence in his apartment that he had destroyed would be obvious.

The mailer he was sending out would not be. It didn't have his name on it, or even his address.

At the end of the hallway, Dino pulled open the chute that had been installed the year before in the building on every floor. It allowed the renters to drop in whatever they wanted mailed, and it would be sent out before the hour was up.

One benefit to paying high maintenance costs, Dino thought.

He dropped the mailer into the slot, hearing it hit the sides of the chute with loud thumps before it finally came to a stop on the bottom floor's mailing cart.

Dino only had the time to close his apartment door when he heard the first bang of boots coming down the hallway.

The officials only had to knock once before he let them in.

CHAPTER 26

"DINO DeLuca," the agent said, strolling into the interrogation room with files in hand. Behind him came another agent, and in his hands he held a familiar garbage can. "How're you feeling, Dino? Comfortable? Hungry? Cigarette?"

Dino flicked the agent with a disinterested look, and then went back to studying the marks on his wrists from the cuffs being put on too tightly. "Fuck off."

"That's not a particularly great way to start this conversation."

"*Please* fuck off," Dino said, not bothering in the slightest to hide his smirk at the anger that flashed in the agent's eyes.

"The hard way it is."

Dino had no idea what the fool was talking about, and while he was sure he wouldn't like it, he wisely chose to stay quiet as the other agent placed the garbage can on the table top. He could see the dusting of ash around the rim, and the marks on the side that said they had tried to get fingerprints off the item.

They didn't need to bother.

He'd tell them it was his. It came from inside his goddamn office.

It wasn't news who it belonged to.

The agents—the same ones who had accosted him outside of his club, Courtly and Stanely—murmured back and forth between one another too low for Dino to hear. He was pretty sure they should have got their act together before they came in to question him, but he didn't care either way.

Finally, Agent Courtly looked to Dino with a smile. "Glad to see they took the cuffs off you."

"I want my lawyer," Dino replied unbothered.

"He's on his way."

"I have nothing to say until he gets here."

"We don't need you to," the agent stated matter-of-fact.

Wonderful.

"As you can see," Agent Stanley said, waving at the cold, gray room, "we've been lucky enough to have been included in a special task force with the Chicago PD in an effort to lower, if not irradiate, the crime problem in Chicago."

Dino scoffed. "That bullshit again?"

The agent barely even blinked. "Yeah, this again."

Agent Courtly patted his partner on the shoulder as he stepped closer to the table. "Fact is, Chicago has been home to the Outfit organization for over eighty years, and over sixty percent of the crime, drug trade, and illegal weapons dealing in this city can be attributed straight back to the mob."

Dino didn't like where this was going.

"Let me guess," he said, glancing up at the ceiling as he placed his hands behind his head, "why bother fidget-fucking with the little guys on the streets when you could take out the big guys and cut the whole problem off at the knees?"

The agent smiled at Dino. "There you go. You're getting it now."

He was, unfortunately.

He liked it even less than he thought he would.

After all, it was *him* in that interrogation room, not another Outfit man, or for that matter, *more* Outfit men.

Dino had been targeted for a reason. He had been pulled in because they had shit—dirt—on him to put him away. It was how these people worked. They wanted an informant, someone to put on the inside and get them the information they wanted, then they picked out the weakest fucking fool in the joint and went after them in whatever way they could.

Usually jail time was a good threat to use.

No man wanted his freedom taken away.

Dino, in that moment, was more concerned with protecting his life.

"So," Dino continued, sitting straight in the chair and resting his arms to the table, "let me get this straight. You have some shit on me that you mean to scare me with—some charges you might be able to trump up for a few years' worth of time behind bars, if you're lucky, though I think it's probably a year at most. See, I know what you likely found in my office and home, which was very fucking little. Let me save you the time and get all of this out of the way."

"Dino," Agent Stanley started to say.

Dino leaned forward in his seat, staring the men in the faces and sneering. "Put me away—file your fucking charges. Get me into arraignment. I'll do general population for a year. Fuck *off*."

Quick as a whip, Agent Courtly hit the corner of the small metal garbage can, letting it topple over across the table. A plume of black ashes wafted out, blowing over Dino's prone form, the table, and the floor. By the time it had settled, he'd breathed in a good dose of the shit, and was covered in it too.

It took every ounce of fucking willpower Dino had not to get up from the table and beat the living hell out of the agent. He decided against the desire, if only because he knew that would earn him a few assault charges.

"Get my lawyer," Dino uttered through clenched teeth.

Neither agent moved an inch.

In fact, the one tossed the file he'd been holding down to the table. Then, he reached over and opened it up fast, causing more ashes to blow all over the place.

How long was Dino going to have to sit through this entire shit show?

Because he was *over* it.

"We warned you last week, didn't we?" Agent Courtly asked quietly.

Dino's brow furrowed, and he clenched his hands under the table in an effort to hide his frustrations. If he didn't do something with his hands, he was going to beat them into the skulls of these idiots. "How many times am I going to have to ask for my—"

"He's coming," the agent barked. "Shut up and listen, DeLuca."

"You've got about ten seconds to talk before I earn myself a few assault charges to go along with whatever other filings you've got ready for me," Dino responded in kind.

He figured the least he could do was warn the fools.

Let them do with it what they wanted.

The agent pulled a piece of paper—one single document—from the opened file on the table, and then tossed it in Dino's general direction. He didn't bother to grab for the paper, instead letting it fall off to the side, sparing it a glance before he looked back to the agents.

"Will you get to the damn point?" Dino demanded.

Agent Stanley passed his partner a look, one that was filled with both exasperation and confusion, before going back to Dino. "We told you last week that someone was out to make a mess for you—we made it very *clear* that you had an option, Dino. All you needed to do was talk, as we were already in the process of digging deeper into the info that had been mailed into our taskforce."

Dino blinked.

Mailed in?

Finally, he looked down to the paper, recognizing it immediately as one of the *several* documents from his club office that had gone missing over the last few months. It wasn't exactly damning—a bank statement from an offshore account that showed money being withdrawn from the offshore account into one of Dino's American bank accounts.

But still, funneling money was illegal.

Dino would need to show where that money came from, where it went to, and where it came out from to show that everything was as legit as it could possibly be. That there was no fraudulent activity to be found in his accounts. That his money was not being made from illegal activities and then pillowed in by legal ventures to hide where it came from.

It was messy.

But it was enough for warrants, he knew. It was enough to open his books.

It was *enough* to start a very long and shitty process that would put him under a microscope for a *very* long time.

"Do you think he's getting it yet?" one of the agents asked the other.

Still, Dino only stared at the document.

Someone had gone into his office, taken his documents, and mailed at least one into a taskforce with some kind of information to start an investigation on him.

Deep down, he knew exactly who had done it.

Ben.

His only question with no answer was *why*.

"I get it," Dino said gruffly, never looking away from the paper.

"Then how about we have a serious discussion about where you can go from here, Dino?" Agent Stanley asked, leaning down on the table with his palms curled around the edge. "We can get you put in a safe position, sweep all of this under the rug—hell, if you need a bit of time behind bars to make it look really good, we can do that, too—and then get you out clean once it is all said and done and we have what we need to kill the Outfit organization if you just *help* us out a little bit.

"We're not asking for much, and we're offering you a pretty good deal. Your father took it once—took it without even thinking about it, or so we were told—once he realized how easy it would be without the mafia running his life."

"My father was killed because of what he did," Dino countered.

Partly, he added silently.

"That was a mistake," one of the two assured, his voice too calm to belie the truth Dino knew was hidden beneath the words.

They called it a mistake.

Fact was, no one, not the mafia or the officials, had ever cared that Dino's father had been killed for turning rat all those years ago. No one gave a single fuck that his mother had been caught up in the end, and killed as well. Not a soul in the world had stopped to look at the three DeLuca children left as orphans because of what everyone liked to say was nothing more than a *mistake*.

"No," Dino murmured firmly.

His answer for that would always be the same.

"Dino, now—"

Dino shook his head. "If the sentiment wasn't heard before, it's not going to change, so let me give you a reminder. It'll be the last thing I have to say to you without my lawyer present. *Fuck off.*"

That finally seemed to do the trick.

Both agents' faces clouded in their anger and frustration, with Courtly being the first agent to stalk back out of the room, slamming the door loudly behind him as he left.

Stanley, on the other hand, stayed behind.

"Can I do something for you?" Dino asked, letting his irritation bleed through in his tone.

"You're really going to take the hell this is going to bring your way, huh?" the agent asked quieter than he had spoken before. "Your whole life is going to be upended, Dino. As of this moment, we have you on two illegal weapons charges due to what we found in your home, and another set of charges we've yet to file for the cooked books related to your club.

"That's going to be a year, at *least*, but shit, we might get you for two, depending on what judge we can pull out of our asses. We're going to make your life a living hell when we tear into each and every single one of your businesses. How many homes do you have—apartments, vacation places? What will we find in those?"

Dino refused to speak or even look at the agent as he talked. He let the man rant on, because he had fuck all to say, or at least, nothing that would do him any good at the moment.

The agent honestly didn't seem to mind.

"I bet we'll find enough," the agent continued on, calm as ever, "it might take a while, no doubt. A couple of years of digging, of going through financials and out of country records, freezing each and every one of your accounts that we can while you're locked away on these first set of charges, but we'll get it done *eventually*. We will have a *stack* of charges waiting for you when you get out this time around, a whole new round of shit to put you away with, and my bet, Dino, is it won't be for a year or two."

Dino swallowed hard, knowing the agent had yet to speak even one lie.

He figured confidence was better than fear at the moment.

Even if it wasn't real.

"My bet," the agent said, turning to leave but looking over his shoulder at Dino as he spoke, "is that we'll put you away for life."

"I welcome your efforts," Dino said, staring the man right in the eye.

"I doubt that, Dino. I believe you already know where you're going in, due time."

He did know, but that didn't mean he had to show it.

"I've already been through hell. Trust me when I say, prison isn't it. Not even a life sentence can compare to the hell I have already lived. Don't try to scare me with that tactic, it's a worthless effort."

Much like his life, sadly.

The agent barely gave a reaction to that, instead, shaking his head with a profound understanding coloring his older features. "I have never fully understood the hold the mafia has on its members, or at least, those we couldn't entice enough with a *free, good* life."

"I don't need you to give me anything," Dino said, shrugging, "I can get the good life all on my own, thanks."

"Take the deal—we'll give you forty-eight hours to decide."

His answer was still the same as it had been minutes before.

It wasn't going to change.

"Fuck off."

CHAPTER 27

THOSE forty-eight hours passed by at a crawling snail's pace. Forty-eight hours of being shuffled from one cell to another in the county jail, of looking new incomers in the eye, and avoiding the splatters of vomit when the drunks finally awoke from their stupors.

Forty-eight hours of asking for his lawyer.

Forty-eight hours of being denied phone calls.

Forty-eight hours of having his rights ignored.

Dino was sure there was some other shit at play with the police, the FBI agents, and even others that he couldn't see, but that didn't make it easier. Each time he approached the row of bars and called out to the guard that he again, wanted his lawyer, and again, wanted his phone calls, he only got a disinterested grunt for a response.

Those forty-eight hours ticked down like a fucking time bomb in the back of Dino's brain. Prison wouldn't be like jail, he knew. He'd have a cell mate, not a half a dozen drunks and a few male prostitutes shoved into the same barred quarters. There would be lights out and yard time, plus that three-meal-a-day guarantee.

It wasn't any of that nonsense that gave Dino cause to pause.

No, it was being locked up that bothered him.

His freedom being taken away.

The inability to up and go when he wanted just because he could. The feeling of being caged crawling over his nervous system one minute, and the anxiety of knowing he couldn't get out was slamming into him like a wrecking ball the next minute.

That was the shit that made him pause.

Made him … consider.

Still, he knew better; knew that taking any sort of deal to turn informant for the FBI or any officials would not end well for him, and so he stopped allowing himself to consider it at all. He didn't sleep those forty-eight hours, not when doing so could mean he'd wake up in the midst of a nightmare and anyone within hearing distance would witness one of his *many* weaknesses in action.

He focused on staying awake, on planning, and a hell of a lot more about Karen.

Had his package arrived yet?

He doubted it, given he'd dropped it in the chute on a Friday, and it was only Sunday evening now. Tomorrow, probably.

He wondered if his face had been splashed across the news, and thought it was likely that it had been, if only because when shit went down in the mafia, the media loved to run with it, spinning the story wildly out of control just to stir up interest and ratings.

Had she seen any of it?

Would she even care if she had?

Scrubbing a hand over his face, Dino leaned against the cinderblock wall and willed away his exhaustion and frustrations. It would do him no good to get lost in that mess, and he sure as hell couldn't afford to sit down if he wanted to stay awake for as long as possible.

He needed to catch bail after he was properly arraigned, but how long was that going to take?

Dino was painfully aware of the fact he had too much negatives stacked up in his favor. He was going to be the victim of his own circumstance when it was all said and done.

He would have no one to blame but himself.

The squeak of Italian leather dress shoes finally made Dino look up from the floor and drop his hand from his face. Throughout his time in the jail, he'd spent far more energy than he wanted to admit paying attention to stupid things just to pass time and keep awake, and one of those things happened to be the sounds of footsteps walking through the halls and outside of the general cells.

Italian leather made a distinct squeak on cheap tiles.

It couldn't be missed.

Not once since he had been brought in had he heard that

sound. No one with a government salary inside the building could afford the Italian leather his family—even himself—wore daily. Not to mention, the guards all wore the same shoes, compliments of a shitty, ugly uniform they were provided with when given the job.

Sure enough, when Dino looked up, he found a familiar sight standing just beyond the cell. Ben DeLuca looked rather smug—and somehow, a little disgusted—peering over the people that shared the space with his nephew.

At the sight of his uncle, Dino's rage only grew from a small fire to a goddamned inferno inside his chest. It only proved his paranoid thinking was probably right, and that Ben likely *did* have something to do with Dino's current predicament.

If nothing else, simply by lending some kind of hand to the officials.

"You look tired, Dino," Ben said. "You've found yourself in a ... *cosa triste, nipote*."

Dino had all he could do to temper his response, his teeth grinding in an effort to hold back what he really wanted to say. "Yes, a *sad thing*, indeed. But did I find myself here, Ben, or was I helped?"

Ben didn't answer that.

Dino wasn't the least bit surprised.

"Where is my lawyer?" Dino asked, his patience lessening. "I've asked for Tony fifty times *today*. You're not Tony."

Ben lifted a single finger high, waving it as if to chide Dino without actually saying something to rebuke him. It was purely instinct and nothing more for Dino to react to that movement, if only because his uncle had used it on more than one occasion before using some sort of violent action toward him. This time was no exception for Dino's reaction as he moved slightly to the side, putting more of his back toward his uncle.

It didn't factor into him at all that they were separated by bars and cement.

It didn't matter that Ben couldn't get inside the cell, not that he would if he were even able.

Dino couldn't help his reactions. They were involuntary.

It was lesson after lesson, literally beaten into his body and mind.

He couldn't wake up one day and forget them.

"Tony works for me, of course," Ben said, smiling slightly and tipping his hand as if to wave off Dino's concerns. "And he doesn't work on weekends."

Dino's jaw clenched. "I pay him."

"That doesn't make you his boss, Dino."

And that, he knew, was the biggest problem of all.

Even his goddamn lawyer couldn't be trusted.

Without fully admitting as much, Ben basically said he was the reason Dino's lawyer had yet to show at the jail. His own *uncle* was holding back his ability to get free.

"Why?" Dino asked quietly.

Ben cocked his head to the side, watching Dino through the bars. "Why what, *nipote?*"

"Why do this, Ben?"

Dino wasn't going to explain himself or his words beyond the question he posed. He figured he wouldn't really have to where Ben was concerned. *If* his uncle was the reason for the official's attention, the raid, and his subsequent arrest, Ben wouldn't need further explanation. He would have an answer at the ready.

And surprise …

His uncle did.

"I tried to make you listen—with the family, with Theo, his friends, other factions. You were too busy, doing what *you* wanted," Ben said, his tone lowering to a darker note as he went along. "I thought a reminder would do you good, but the first lesson apparently didn't *take*. Perhaps I've been going about teaching you and Theo the wrong way all these years. Would a *time out* work better for you, Dino? Will putting you away where you can't make choices I don't approve and mess with my plans when you're not to touch them, help you any? We'll certainly see now, won't we?"

"You had me *arrested* because of *Theo?*" Dino snarled, pushing away from the wall and moving closer to where his uncle stood behind the bars.

Ben didn't look the least bit affected by Dino's anger.

What concerns should he have with Dino safe behind bars?

None.

Once again, Ben had the control.

Once again, Ben pulled the strings.

Once again, Ben made the calls.

Dino was just the sorry fucking fool who happened to be

caught up in whatever games Ben felt like playing because he could.

Nothing more.

Just because he *could.*

In that moment, as he stared at his uncle and Ben stared back, still smiling in that amused, cold way of his, Dino realized it was as if time had suddenly hit the rewind button without any notice at all. He felt as though he were once again a young man, stuck under his uncle's thumb and control because of what he thought at the time was circumstance, but actually proved to be because of Ben's own meddling and wants.

Just like when his parents' had been murdered by his uncle, Dino was forced into Ben's life whether he wanted to be there or not, doing what his uncle demanded he do because if he didn't, he would eventually learn what pain truly was when he refused.

This very situation was no different.

A new punishment, yes.

The outcome—the *pain*—would be no different.

"It helps to have friends in many places," Ben noted, glancing over his shoulder at a guard that strolled on by without even giving the two a bit of his attention. It was almost as if Ben wasn't there at all to the man. "Make a few calls, transfer a bit of cash … and look what we have, my nephew without any sort of help."

"Is the FBI one of those friends, too?" Dino asked.

"Friends *of* friends, perhaps. It's not important. This will do you well, Dino. A little time out will do you good."

Dino's gaze narrowed.

Ben had no idea what he had done. He didn't even understand that his little trick—his lesson, whatever it was—had started a small avalanche of circumstances for Dino that would not be fixed with a little *time out* as his uncle liked to say. It was not that simple.

"You did this to me because of *Theo*," Dino repeated.

Ben shrugged. "Theo was the tip of a floating iceberg. The most dangerous part of an iceberg is what we cannot see of it, Dino. But as the tip of the iceberg, you're also entirely unneeded— a waste, really. Something disposable, replaceable even."

And that was exactly the problem, Dino knew.

He would always be nothing more than *waste* to his uncle.

A man with no worth.

Wasted worth for that matter, as Ben's only effort where Dino was concerned had always been to manipulate, to abuse, and to use.

"If you were willing to begin defying me on something like your brother and what I wanted from him, as you did when you were younger, and if I allowed that to continue, what would happen, hmm?" Ben asked. "Tell me."

Dino knew the answer all too well.

He would have continued to defy Ben.

He had already been doing so over and over.

Ben was just cutting off the problem at the knees before it could grow into something he couldn't control.

Problem was, Ben didn't realize his own mistake in what he'd done.

This time, he'd pushed Dino a little too far.

This time, Dino had far more to lose.

More than Theo.

More than his sister Lily.

Dino had things to fight for, now.

He wasn't going to take this lying down.

It might take a little while, sure. Dino had every reason to believe he wouldn't be able to do much while he was behind bars, especially if Ben was working to make damn sure he stayed right where he was for as long as possible.

Dino could wait.

He'd been waiting for a long time, anyway.

Ben rapped his knuckles on the bars, smiling again. "Enjoy your time away. Tony will see you on Monday at your arraignment."

"Go to hell, Ben."

His uncle walked away *laughing*.

CHAPTER 28

DINO attempted, and failed, to straighten out his crumpled looking suit jacket after the cuffs had been taken off and he was directed to sit with a row of waiting people. Other detainees waiting who were also at the courthouse for their arraignment.

His lawyer had yet to show, though Dino wasn't surprised.

Opting to stand against the wall while guards patrolled the hallway, Dino stared out the window at the bright sun, his fatigue fading for a brief moment. It was long enough for him to think he might actually be able to make it through this godforsaken day.

If anything, he'd be able to stay awake while the sun was high.

It was only the shout of his name that took his attention away from the sun and the brief bit of comfort it provided. To his left, Dino found his brother jogging toward him, and another man close behind him. Damian Rossi.

"Dino, shit …" Theo maneuvered his way past the guard, a garment bag in hand, and passed it over to his brother. "Tony is almost here."

Dino wished that would make a difference for him.

It wouldn't.

He took the garment bag from his brother, finding a clean blazer and silk shirt inside. Uncaring that people were watching, he quickly changed clothes, though a guard stepped forward to check his items to make sure he wasn't handing something over, before Theo could take the dirty stuff.

"Thank you," Dino said to his brother.

Sometimes, a clean shirt made all the difference to a man's

attitude.

Theo shrugged. "Not a big deal."

Yeah, it was.

The brothers weren't friends, not *really*.

Theo didn't have to be there.

Honestly, he shouldn't have been there at all.

Dino was still grateful that he was.

Damian Rossi, however, was another story.

"Brought your friend along for a show?" Dino asked, nodding in Damian's direction.

The man stood a few feet back, out of earshot of the conversation, but still close enough that he could step forward and join if he wanted to.

"What?" Theo asked.

"Never mind."

Dino didn't share the closeness with Damian that Theo did. When the two men were younger, Damian and Theo were practically inseparable, and they often added little Lily to the mix as well. He supposed it wasn't his place to question it all.

Theo stared down the long hallway, keeping his gaze anywhere but Dino. He understood his brother's distance, as he too tried to maintain the same aloof attitude, though his was not as much of a façade as his brother's was.

Theo simply needed someone to break through his walls.

Dino could never let his walls down.

"Hey," Dino said, gaining Theo's attention, "do me a favor?"

"Sure."

"Keep an eye on Lily for me, check up on where she is in Europe from time to time, send her cash if she needs it, or whatever. She's probably going to think I'm ignoring her or—"

"I can let her know what's going on with you," Theo interrupted quietly.

Dino shook his head. "I don't want her to know."

He didn't want his younger sister coming back home for him, because he knew what would happen if she did step foot back on US soil. Their uncle would get his claws into her, and there she would be, fucked and stuck doing whatever the hell Ben demanded.

As long as Lily was out of reach for Ben, she would continue to be okay.

Dino needed to make sure that happened for her.

His sister might not understand his silence, she might even think he'd forgotten about her, and the festering bitterness she already felt about their life, the mafia, and the death of their parents might grow into something larger than her already small life.

It was a risk Dino was willing to take.

For his siblings, he'd risk everything.

"Don't tell her," Dino repeated, "just keep her where she is, Theo."

Theo nodded. "All right."

"And get out of here. You don't need to be here for this."

"But—"

Dino waved a hand at his brother, knowing damn well he probably looked cold as hell doing so. It didn't matter, he would do what he needed to do to keep his siblings safe, especially from Ben's ire. He had no doubt Ben had told Theo to stay away from Dino during any legal proceedings or what was yet to come.

Between the two brothers, Theo didn't like to follow the rules.

Dino was always covering in one way or another for his brother.

This time would be no exception.

"Go," Dino muttered, glancing away from his brother. "I've got this shit handled."

"Do you?"

"I will."

His assurance didn't come out as strongly as he wanted it to, but what could Dino do?

Nothing.

Wait it out, he told himself.

Soon, Theo was gone, and Damian followed close behind his friend. Dino didn't even get the chance to settle back and relax before his lawyer finally decided to make his appearance known. Flashing a courthouse badge at the guard, Dino was allowed to leave the other people waiting, and he followed behind the well-dressed, stoutly lawyer who hadn't even bothered to bring his briefcase along with him.

He wouldn't need it.

Dino might have been paying him, but he knew now that Tony was on someone else's payroll—Ben.

Tony would do what Ben wanted, not what was best for

Dino.

Hard choices sometimes needed to be made when someone couldn't afford to cash the check they would be left with after it was all said and done. This was going to be one of those times for Dino. He would handle it as he needed to, but he had a few things he had to do first.

"Well," Tony said, his voice a droning yawn, as he pulled out a chair to sit in the private room they'd been directed to, "what of it, Dino?"

Dino stared hard at the lawyer. "You're the professional, you tell me."

"Few charges, nothing serious. You can do the time."

A scoff worked its way up Dino's throat, but somehow, he managed to hold it back.

"That's it?" Dino asked. "I can do the time. You're not even going to suggest we work on some kind of deal with the prosecution to ease this a bit?"

"You're not the kind of man who works *deals*."

That much was true.

But Tony *was* the kind of lawyer who could do it on the low.

In fact, he'd done it for Dino before on other minor charges, and for Ben on bigger charges. This shouldn't have been a huge thing to ask for.

"Or Ben told you not to bother," Dino said.

Tony looked up from the table. "Hmm, what?"

Exactly.

"I need to make a phone call," Dino said, refusing to repeat what he knew Tony had heard him say loud and clear. "They won't give me the chance to at the jail, always spitting out one excuse after the other. Give me your phone so I can make a call."

Tony pushed his cell phone down the table, seemingly unbothered by the request. Dino snatched it up, typing in a familiar number on the touch screen and then putting the phone to his ear when it started to ring through.

There were many people he could have called.

He even knew a few lawyers on hand that might be able to pull strings for him.

None of it would really help.

Dino had already come to a sad understanding of where he was going to be staying for the next little while, and his phone use would be monitored, if not limited. He couldn't be making *this* kind of call and request on a jail phone.

Finally, five *long* rings later, the boss picked up.

"*Ciao,*" Terrance Trentini greeted cheerfully.

Dino swallowed back the ire that caused to boil in his stomach—the jealous swell of how easily others overlooked his situation time and time again. No doubt, Terrance was just another one of those people pretending like he didn't know what was happening to Dino at the moment.

"Boss," Dino replied as respectfully as he could manage. "I'd like to put that request in for my brother to get his title."

It took a good thirty seconds before Terrance responded.

"Dino."

"Who else?"

Terrance laughed, though the sound was false and weak. "I heard you got mixed up in some trouble. You shouldn't be calling me."

"Using a safe phone, boss."

"Ah."

"That request," Dino prodded, "for Theo. I want to make it happen."

"I'm not sure—"

"I need someone looking after my crew and shit for the next little while. I don't want someone appointed to it, and certainly not someone Ben dreams up for the job. My brother can do it—he's *been* doing it. You said when I gave the okay, you would do it. I'm giving my okay. Give him the title."

"Your uncle doesn't seem to think Theo is ready for it."

"I do," Dino replied.

Tony had listened to the conversation without saying a word, but Dino believed wholeheartedly that the lawyer would be making a phone call to his uncle once he was done with Dino. It didn't even matter. This wasn't about Ben DeLuca. This wasn't about Dino.

It was for Theo.

It would be a good, sturdy position for Theo to have when his brother was locked behind bars, unable to lend a voice of authority for his younger brother's sake.

Dino had habits he couldn't break, no matter how hard he tried.

Caring for his siblings was just one of them.

Even when they didn't know he was doing it.

"I'll owe you," Dino said, offering the words easily, though it wasn't something he handed out to any man in the mafia. No one wanted to be in someone else's debt. Especially not a boss's debt. He would do it for his brother, though. "Whatever you need, boss."

Terrance sighed. "The charges are that serious?"

"Some haven't been officially filed yet, while others have, but yes."

"Fine."

Dino couldn't help but wonder … "You're not the least bit concerned that I'll come out of this like my father did—a rat?"

Terrance laughed again, loud and hard. "Dino … that is the *one* thing I have never worried myself over where you and your brother are concerned. You're not your father—your uncle made sure of that."

Dino wasn't so sure.

And he certainly wouldn't give credit to his uncle, either.

After a quick goodbye, Dino slid the phone back to the lawyer. Tony pocketed the device, looking to Dino expectantly.

"Happy?" the lawyer asked.

Not yet.

"You're fired," Dino said.

Tony's eyes grew as wide as saucers. "I beg your pardon?"

Dino waved at the door behind him. "Take me back to where the others are waiting for their public defenders to show up. I'll take their lead and grab myself one appointed by the court. I don't need another one of Ben's underlings fucking me around more than he already has—that includes you, Tony. Get out. You're fired."

"A *public defender?*" the lawyer asked, his face reddening.

Dino laughed at the sight of the man's rage.

He'd take the time that was thrown at him. He already knew he wasn't going to be given bail, as he'd be considered a major fucking flight risk, what with his connections out of country and the proof the prosecution would have about his overseas bank accounts in countries that had no extradition treaties with the United States.

Dino was good and fucked, and nobody had even thought to

use lube when they bent him over. But he'd take it.

What else could he do? He'd do what he needed to do.

God save their souls when he was out, though. He planned on coming out swinging.

"You're serious," Tony spluttered in his outrage.

"Anyone will be better than *you*."

He fucking meant it, too.

CHAPTER 29

THE bespectacled, gangly man peered over the documents, and then looked to Dino. Over the period of a few weeks, he had learned a few things about his public defender—Mike, the guy liked to be called—that he thought was most noteworthy. The man was young—twenty-seven, to be exact—for a lawyer, but he'd earned his degrees, without question. He never questioned Dino's requests, and not once had he asked Dino if he was *really* guilty.

That gained the guy brownie points.

"You're serious about this?" Mike asked.

"They offered it, didn't they?"

Mike nodded, going back to the documents. Dino took the time to look around the room they were in, noting the gray walls and barred windows. The jail gave very little by way of comfort, and Dino had called this place home for four long weeks.

He had a while yet to go, though.

"It'll be a year and a half if you plead guilty on the gun charges and the possession charges they added on for the five ounces of weed they picked up in your office," Mike explained.

"Five ounces they planted," Dino muttered.

All the drugs had been cleared out.

Theo made sure of it the week before the raid.

No matter, what was done was done.

"Plead on these now, and they'll drop the fraud, laundering, and tax evasion charges," the public defender added, not that Dino needed him to.

He was already well aware of the deal that had been put on

the table.

"If nothing else, it'll offer you a bit of time outside prison before they build that case," Mike said, glancing to Dino.

"Is it that they don't have the evidence they need yet to get the verdict on those charges, or they just want to play keep-away with my freedom?" Dino asked.

Mike shrugged. "Both?"

"Fucking fantastic."

"You can be out in a year—maybe—on good behavior."

Dino glanced out the barred window as he said, "Yeah, I got it, Mike."

"You ready to make that deal?"

No.

No, he was not.

It was one thing for a made man to plead no contest in court, but it was another thing for him to be found guilty, or plead guilty. It just didn't look good for his reputation with the family. Not that being arrested looked good as it was, because that was just a whole other mess to deal with once a man was free.

Thankfully, it looked like Dino would have some time to consider all of that.

That time would be spent in a very small cell.

Dino knew he really didn't have a choice but to take the deal that was offered—he was a small fish, to be sure, but all the original charges had been stacked against him, even the fraud, tax evasion, and laundering, and the prosecution had done just what he knew they would and argued he was a flight risk.

So there he was, denied bail on a goddamn drug and weapons charges because *now* they were going to drop the other charges that had actually been the point in context for his denied freedom while he awaited trial. In doing so, he was now being given a deal that would immediately put his plea in, speed up his court dates which would not offer him another bail hearing, and he'd be looking at his new jail cell within the week.

That was how fast they wanted him put away.

Dino could do nothing about it.

Fuck the people who had done this to him.

Fuck them all.

"Give me the papers," Dino said gruffly, not wanting to stay lost in his thoughts for too long lest he let them overwhelm his apathy. Once he got angry, it seemed like lately that was all he could feel when it came on. And shit, he wanted to *feed* it something bad. "I'll sign right now—get this fucking shit over with."

"You'll have some time out of prison before they bring the second round," Mike said again, "and it'll give you time to plan."

"Also gives them time to royally screw me over more than they already have."

Mike didn't deny it.

"Then why sign?" his lawyer asked as he handed the papers over.

For a single second, as Dino's hand hovered over the deal the prosecution had painstakingly detailed in twenty printed pages back and front, he hesitated in signing.

No, that wasn't entirely truthful.

He hesitated in answering Mike's question and answering it *honestly*.

Staring across the metal table, Dino met his lawyer's gaze. "Let me ask you a question."

"Shoot. We've got all the time in the world."

Unfortunately.

"Have you been approached by anyone yet?" Dino asked.

Mike instantly leaned back in his seat, his fingers steepling as he considered Dino's question. "You know, I've been good, Dino, as far as you're concerned. I didn't ask if you were guilty, I didn't question you on your involvement with the mafia or your connections in that regard—none of it."

"But you *want* to," Dino pressed.

"Is it going to let me defend you any better than I can now?"

"No."

Mike pointed at him. "Exactly—no. And that's why I haven't asked. I might be just a public defender, bottom of the barrel to some, but there's a reason why you picked a public defender. I was just the lucky fucker that got appointed to your case, it could have just as easily been Margie in the next office, but no, it was me that got the draw. There's a reason you went with a public defender, my friend, but I haven't asked."

"You're not on a payroll," Dino said honestly.

"I'm not. And no, Dino, I haven't been approached or threatened or sent a message, to answer that for you, too. Might as well get it out of the way."

That was music to Dino's ears.

"Good."

"So tell me," Mike said, leaning forward, "why sign?"

"They're going to draw this out," Dino said, "they've already got me on a denied bail, and if I don't sign, I might get another bail hearing whenever the hell the judge feels like signing off on a date for another hearing, but it could be a month or more for that. By then, they'll refile the other charges, and that'll be yet another argument on why I can't get bail because I have every resource at my fingertips to *run*."

"But they might not have a strong enough case on the other charges," Mike suggested.

"Might," Dino agreed, "but that's not a risk I'm willing to take. Look at it like this, they can draw this out for a good six months, maybe more, before any real movement is going to happen. Or I can take this deal, do my year and a half—maybe a year if I'm lucky—get out, and resume my life for a bit. It'll give me a chance to explain myself, to do what I should have done before I got put in here like this."

"They're going to put you back in, though."

Dino nodded once. "But it'll give me time, Mike. I only need time."

For Karen.

For his unborn child.

For his siblings.

For the Outfit.

Dino only needed just a small bit of time on his side to do what he needed to do, and he'd do it damn well.

"Take the deal, then?" Mike asked.

Dino signed his name across the dotted line, flipped a page, and signed another piece. He continued this until each and every page had his name written on it, signaling he fully understood what he was agreeing to, and would make every effort to do as the prosecution wanted him to when he was brought back into the courts.

When he had finished, Dino pushed the papers back over to Mike who took them with a sad smile.

"One other thing," Mike said as he stood from the table.

Dino crossed his arms, staring out at the door where he knew a guard would come to get him to return him to a cell as soon as Mike was gone. "What's that, man?"

"They tell me you're not using a phone and you've had no visitors."

All true.

"What about it?" Dino asked.

"You don't have someone you want to call or talk to? Someone you'd like to see?"

Dino frowned before he could stop himself.

His answer to those questions were an absolutely empathetic *yes*.

Every day, he thought of Karen. Every day, he hurt.

Every day, he reminded himself of *why* he was doing what he was doing, and that while it would hurt her—while she would probably never understand—he was doing it so that she was safe, and she would remain so.

It barely helped.

His heart still felt blackened, burned, and ruined.

He was reduced back to that worthless, black existence that had become a faithful friend before Karen came along.

"Is this like the public defender thing?" Mike asked, clearly choosing his words carefully.

Dino appreciated the effort. "Sort of, but—"

"I can do whatever you want or ask me to do as long as it's not illegal, Dino."

"Shit, some lawyers will even do the illegal stuff for you."

Mike smirked at his joke. "Not me, though."

"This isn't that."

"What is it?" the lawyer asked.

Dino took a breath in, wishing his chest didn't feel so heavy but empty at the same time. "It's complicated, is all."

"You were a complicated case."

"It's not entirely over yet," he reminded the lawyer.

Mike agreed to that statement. "But what about *this*— whatever it is?"

Dino looked over to the door again—it was still closed as Mike hadn't pressed the buzzer yet. There were no cameras or wires in the room recording their conversation because of attorney and client privilege prevented the jail from doing so.

It was a small gift, if nothing else.

"Dino," Mike pressed gently, "I was only given an hour."

Dino was aware.

"Her name is Karen," Dino said quietly, "and she's another reason I needed to settle this out now, because her name is on a few things I don't want them digging into, and it might give my guys some time to wash away what might come up for her on one of my businesses that they haven't dug into yet."

Mike's head cocked to the side, his confusion evident. "What does she have—"

"She's pregnant with my child, and I've kept her presence a secret from people in my family who might do her harm. Because that's exactly what they would do to her if they knew—harm her."

The lawyer took his seat again, not saying a word as he did so.

Dino sympathized with the man. It was a lot to take in, but he thought maybe—*God*, maybe—this was one more way for him to *keep* Karen. If only he could explain … talk to her, even if it was through someone else … if only …

It was selfish. Purely for his own wants. He should let her go, let her mend whatever heartbreak he'd caused her and hope that she would do better—be better—without him. She could be better, he knew, but he was *that* selfish.

"I don't know how much, if anything, she knows about my legal problems," Dino said, "as we didn't end this on good terms, and I basically left her hanging in the wind. She's going to have the baby before I even get out—if I get the full year and a half, the baby will be a year old by the time I even get to meet him or her."

Mike cleared his throat and scrubbed a hand through his hair. "Huh."

"*If* I get to meet the baby," Dino corrected quieter, "because who the fuck knows if she'll even want a part in this mess, right?"

"So what do you want me to do to help you with her exactly?" Mike asked.

Dino had kept his shaking hands hidden under the table, or tucked under his crossed arms throughout the whole conversation, as he didn't like to show his weaknesses like they were simply cards for someone else to pick up and use whenever they wanted.

Yet, when Mike asked him—no further explanations needed—what he could do to help, Dino showed his shaking hands, reaching into the pocket of his jail appointed uniform to pull out a stack of papers he'd kept folded up and hidden there. It was only a few, but it was a few pages worth of his soul—blackened, burned, and ruined—scribbled there for Karen.

If she wanted to read.

If she would even *care*.

"There on the top—that's her address," Dino said, handing it over. "I just need you to mail it, no return sender."

Mike took the folded up papers. "That's it?"

Dino shrugged. "The words inside will do the rest."

He hoped …

Time would tell.

It was looking as if he would have a lot of time while he waited.

ABOUT THE AUTHOR

Bethany-Kris is a Canadian author, lover of much, and mother to three very young sons, one cat, and two dogs. A small town in Eastern Canada where she was born and raised is where she has always called home. With her boys under her feet, a snuggling cat, barking dogs, and a spouse calling over his shoulder, she is nearly always writing something ... when she can find the time.

Find Bethany-Kris at:
Her website www.bethanykris.com,
or on Facebook at www.facebook.com/bethanykriswrites,
on her blog at www.bethanykris.com/blog,
or on Twitter - @BethanyKris.

Sign up to Bethany-Kris's New Release Newsletter here:
http://eepurl.com/bf9lzD.

COMING SOON

Worth of Waste
DeLuca Duet, Part Two
Releasing February 6th, 2017

The Chicago Mob is the same as it has always been—violent, greedy, and excessive. The Outfit families have turned their backs when they were needed the most one too many times, but Dino DeLuca didn't expect anything different.

His whole life has been lived for the Outfit—for his family.

He has a whole new set of reasons to live and fight now.

Karen Martin makes Dino change all the rules.

He's finally ready to show everyone just how much waste is truly worth in the mafia, and just how far one will go for freedom from it all.

He's learned these lessons well.

Too well.

Author's Note: The DeLuca Duet is a standalone duet with a HEA ending that can be read independently.

OTHER BOOKS

Filthy Marcellos

Antony
Lucian
Giovanni
Dante
Legacy
The Complete Collection

The Chicago War

Deathless & Divided
Reckless & Ruined
Scarless & Sacred
Breathless & Bloodstained

The Russian Guns

The Arrangement
The Life
The Score
Demyan & Ana
Shattered
The Jersey Vignettes

Find more on Bethany-Kris's website at www.bethanykris.com.